SKELETON CREEK

☠ THE ☠
CROSSBONES

PATRICK CARMAN's
SKELETON CREEK
☠ THE ☠
CROSSBONES

SCHOLASTIC PRESS
NEW YORK

PC STUDIO

Copyright © 2010 by PC Studio, Inc.

All rights reserved. Published by Scholastic Press, an imprint of Scholastic Inc., *Publishers since 1920.* SCHOLASTIC, SCHOLASTIC PRESS, and associated logos are trademarks and/or registered trademarks of Scholastic Inc.

Library of Congress Cataloging-in-Publication Data Available
ISBN 978-0-545-24994-2

10 9 8 7 6 5 4 3 2 1   10 11 12 13 14

Printed in the U.S.A.   23
First edition, September 2010

The text type was set in GFY Thornesmith.
Book design by Christopher Stengel

The text was set in GFY Thornesmith.
Book design by Christopher Stengel
Illustrations by Joshua Pease and Squire Broel

For JT, Josh, and Ben. Telling Ryan's story would be impossible without you.

Special thanks to David Levithan, Jeffrey Townsend, Joshua Pease, Benjamin Apel, and Eric Rhode

SKELETON CREEK
☠ THE ☠
CROSSBONES

MONDAY, JUNE 20, MIDNIGHT

A COUPLE OF DAYS AGO I WALKED PAST A PARKED CAR I'D NEVER SEEN BEFORE. THE OWNER HAD SLAPPED A CROOKED BLUE BUMPER STICKER ON THE TRUNK.

JUST BECAUSE YOU'RE PARANOID DOESN'T MEAN PEOPLE AREN'T REALLY OUT TO GET YOU.

I HAVE NEVER READ A TRUER STATEMENT IN MY LIFE.

MONDAY, JUNE 20, 12:03 A.M.

I AM SURE SOMEONE OR SOMETHING IS OUT TO GET ME. WHATEVER IT IS ESCAPED FROM THE ABANDONED DREDGE AND HAS LEAKED OUT INTO THE REST OF THE WORLD.

It's LOOSE, IT'S ANGRY, AND IT'S LOOKING FOR ME.

I HAVE A BAD HABIT OF ALLOWING THOUGHTS LIKE THIS TO FILL MY MIND IN THE MIDDLE OF THE NIGHT.

IT WANTS TO GET ME.

THERE WAS A TIME WHEN I THOUGHT I TURNED TERRIBLE THINGS OVER IN MY MIND BECAUSE I READ AND WROTE TOO MANY SCARY STORIES. (NOTE TO SELF: START WRITING ABOUT UNICORNS AND BUNNIES.) THE LOGIC WAS PRETTY STRAIGHTFORWARD: I READ ABOUT ZOMBIES, THEREFORE I DREAMT ABOUT WALKING DEAD PEOPLE WITH ARMS THAT FELL OFF. I WROTE STORIES ABOUT GHOSTLY BEINGS, SO NATURALLY I ASSUMED SOMETHING CREEPY WAS STANDING OUTSIDE MY WINDOW WITH A CHAIN SAW.

IT'S A GOOD THING I'M OLDER NOW. I'M WISER. I'VE GOT A BETTER SENSE OF HUMOR. I CAN HANDLE WHATEVER COMES MY WAY.

But this is <u>real</u>, and I can prove it.

You'll see. I'll <u>make</u> you see.

I just thought of a sick story about a giant red bunny and a one-eyed unicorn.

Hang on.

MONDAY, JUNE 20, 1:15 A.M.

OKAY, I'M BACK. AND BUMMED OUT. SOMETIMES THE IDEA FOR A STORY IS SO MUCH BETTER THAN THE STORY ITSELF. SUCH IS THE CASE WITH A ONE-EYED UNICORN GOING TOE-TO-TOE AGAINST A SEVEN-FOOT RABBIT-MAN. THEN AGAIN, DARK HUMOR IS LIKE BLACK MEDICINE FOR MY FEARS. IT KEEPS ME FROM SCREAMING IN THE LONELY HOURS OF THE NIGHT.

MOVING ON . . .

I FEEL I SHOULD RECAP WHAT GOT ME INTO THIS MESS IN THE FIRST PLACE. IT'S GOOD SHORT STORY PRACTICE, IF NOTHING ELSE.

FIRST, THE SEVEN-WORD VERSION:
HAUNTED BY GHOST, FOUND GOLD, SAVED TOWN.

AND THE SLIGHTLY EXPANDED, FAR MORE USEFUL VERSION:
MY BEST FRIEND, SARAH, AND I DISCOVERED THE PRESENCE OF A GHOST OUT IN THE WOODS. THE GHOST WAS CALLED OLD JOE BUSH, AND IT WAS REAL. THE

WOODS WERE HOME TO AN ABANDONED DREDGE, WHICH WAS HAUNTED BY THE GHOST AND PROTECTED BY A SECRET SOCIETY CALLED THE CROSSBONES. MY DAD WAS A CROSSBONES MEMBER, THOUGH I QUESTION TO THIS DAY HOW MUCH HE REALLY KNEW. A CERTAIN SOMEONE I WILL NOT NAME (HIS NAME IS FORBIDDEN IN SKELETON CREEK) WENT TO GREAT LENGTHS TO KEEP PEOPLE AWAY FROM THE DREDGE. HE WENT SO FAR AS TO EMBODY THE GHOST OF OLD JOE BUSH, AND I'M CONVINCED HE WENT CRAZY IN THE EFFORT. AFTER A WHOLE LOT OF INVESTIGATING AND ONE MAJOR INJURY, SARAH AND I DISCOVERED THE REASON WHY THE DREDGE WAS BEING PROTECTED: ITS FLOORBOARDS WERE FILLED WITH FORTY MILLION DOLLARS' WORTH OF GOLD. SARAH AND I WERE CREDITED WITH FINDING THIS LONG-LOST STASH AND WERE FORGIVEN OUR TRANSGRESSIONS, LIKE LYING IN THE FIRST DEGREE, SNEAKING AROUND BEHIND OUR PARENTS' BACKS, ACTING LIKE RECKLESS TEENAGERS, NEARLY GETTING KILLED. THE GHOST OF OLD JOE BUSH IS GONE NOW. IT TOOK THE IMPOSTER AND THE CROSSBONES WITH IT.

I DON'T KNOW WHY I'M WRITING ALL THIS DOWN AFTER ONE IN THE MORNING. FOR ALL I KNOW THE

GHOST OF OLD JOE BUSH IS STANDING IN MY DRIVEWAY, THINKING ABOUT HIS OPTIONS: RIP THE FRONT DOOR OFF ITS RUSTY HINGES? OR QUIETLY WALK THROUGH THE WALLS AND HOVER OVER MY BED?

I AM GOING TO CLOSE MY EYES.

I CAN DO THIS. I CAN GO TO SLEEP. I CAN TURN MY MIND TOWARD SOMETHING OTHER THAN THE GHOST OF OLD JOE BUSH.

I AM THINKING HAPPY BUNNY THOUGHTS.

I ALWAYS FEEL BETTER IN THE MORNING, LIKE THE LIGHT OF DAY HAS TRAPPED MY FEARS UNDER A PILE OF DIRT. AT LEAST THEY'RE BURIED UNTIL NIGHTFALL.

IT'S OFFICIALLY SUMMER, I HAVE A LITTLE BIT OF CASH, AND I LOVE EGGS AND HASH BROWNS. THESE FACTS HAVE DRIVEN ME OUT OF MY BEDROOM AND INTO A BOOTH AT THE CAFÉ ON MAIN STREET. I'VE EMPTIED MY POCKETS ONTO THE SCUFFED GREEN TABLE AND TAKEN STOCK OF MY PATHETIC FINANCIAL CONDITION: TWELVE DOLLARS, FIFTY-FIVE CENTS. AND I DON'T GET ANOTHER INFUSION OF MOOLA UNTIL FRIDAY.

HOW CAN I HAVE A GIANT PILE OF MONEY IN THE BANK AND BE SO BROKE AT THE SAME TIME?

GOOD QUESTION.

THE TOWN GOT MOST OF THE GOLD ME AND SARAH FOUND, WHICH WAS FAIR, I SUPPOSE. THE UNFAIR PART? WHAT GOLD I <u>DID</u> GET TO KEEP WAS PLACED IN A TRUST. I CAN'T TOUCH IT UNTIL I TURN EIGHTEEN, WHICH FEELS LIKE A MILLION YEARS FROM NOW.

WHAT THIS MEANS IS TECHNICALLY MY SOCIAL STATUS HAS GONE <u>DOWN</u> SINCE I SAVED THE TOWN FROM RUIN. EVERYONE ELSE IN SKELETON CREEK IS EITHER

7

DRIVING A NEW PICKUP TRUCK, RENOVATING A HOUSE, OR HAULING A BIG-SCREEN TV THROUGH THE FRONT DOOR. A FAIR NUMBER ARE DOING ALL THREE AT THE SAME TIME.

THE SPENDING SPREE IS COURTESY OF MAYOR BLAKE, WHO'S NEVER LIFTED A FINGER TO DO MUCH OF ANYTHING BESIDES OPEN A PEPSI CAN. HE GAVE EVERY FAMILY, INCLUDING MY OWN, ONE HUNDRED THOUSAND DOLLARS. HE CALLED IT A "STIMULUS PACKAGE" AND ENCOURAGED EVERYONE TO BLOW IT AS FAST AS THEY COULD. ONE THING ABOUT MAYOR BLAKE — HE'S GOOD AT FIRING OFF HIS MOUTH AND GETTING EVERYONE EXCITED. WHETHER IT'S TURNING THE DREDGE INTO A HAUNTED ATTRACTION OR BUILDING A NEW VISITORS' CENTER, THE GUY CAN REALLY YACK IT UP. PEOPLE AROUND HERE ARE PERPLEXED BY SO MUCH CHATTER; IT CONFUSES THEM INTO DOING STUPID THINGS (LIKE SPENDING A HUNDRED GRAND IN NO TIME FLAT).

EVEN AFTER THEY GAVE ME AND SARAH A BIGGER WAD OF DOUGH THAN ANYONE ELSE GOT, THERE WAS STILL MORE THAN TEN MILLION LEFT. A LOT OF NEW FOLKS ARE RUNNING FOR MAYOR SO THEY CAN DECIDE HOW TO SPEND IT, AND THE POPULATION HAS BALLOONED FROM

SEVEN HUNDRED TO SEVEN HUNDRED AND FOURTEEN, A REVERSAL OF DECADES IN THE OTHER DIRECTION.

SITTING IN THE CAFÉ, SIPPING A COLD CUP OF COFFEE, MY THOUGHTS HAVE TURNED TO SARAH. WE USED TO START EVERY SUMMER WITH PLANS ABOUT WHAT KIND OF TROUBLE WE WERE GOING TO GET INTO.

BUT THAT'S GOING TO BE A LITTLE CHALLENGING THIS TIME AROUND, BECAUSE NOW SARAH'S GONE.

I GUESS HER PARENTS LOOKED AT THE MONEY AS A TICKET OUT OF SKELETON CREEK, BECAUSE THEIR HOUSE WAS UP FOR SALE THE SAME DAY THE CHECKS LEFT THE MAYOR'S OFFICE. I DON'T KNOW — I GUESS I CAN HARDLY BLAME THEM. IT'S STILL A DEAD-END TOWN, AND ME AND SARAH DIDN'T EXACTLY GIVE THEM A LOT OF REASONS TO HANG AROUND. ALMOST GETTING KILLED WITH YOUR BEST FRIEND DOES SEND UP A LITTLE BIT OF A RED FLAG. IT WOULDN'T SURPRISE ME IF MY PARENTS AND HER PARENTS HAD A SECRET MEETING.

MY DAD: ONE OF US IS GOING TO HAVE TO MOVE OUT OF TOWN BEFORE OUR KIDS GET THEMSELVES KILLED.

SARAH'S DAD: I'VE GOT FAMILY IN BOSTON. I COULD FIND WORK THERE.

MY DAD: I'D LIKE TO OPEN A FLY SHOP, MAKE A GO OF IT.

SARAH'S DAD: I'LL TALK TO MY WIFE.

I BET THAT'S EXACTLY HOW IT WENT DOWN, FOLLOWED BY A FOR SALE SIGN POUNDED INTO THE MUD IN FRONT OF HER HOUSE.

WITH SARAH GONE, THINGS CHANGED. WE EMAILED AND TALKED TO EACH OTHER ONLINE, BUT THE MESSAGES THINNED TO A FEW LINES HERE AND THERE.

THREE MONTHS AFTER SHE LEFT, I GOT A NOTE THAT FELT LIKE THE BEGINNING OF THE END.

Hey, Ryan,

I was accepted into summer film school at UCLA, so at least I'll be back on the West Coast for a week. I never thought I'd escape Skeleton Creek. I know how it feels there.

Get out or get dead — that's my advice.

S.

It was just the kind of email I didn't need. Not only had Sarah escaped Skeleton Creek without me, but to make matters worse, she felt sorry for me. Get out or get dead? Wow, talk about a two-by-four in the face. That one hurt.

Still, I really miss her. She filled a lot of space, and that space has turned empty.

This is probably why the summer feels so aimless. Our plans were never really <u>our</u> plans. They were <u>her</u> plans.

I have no idea what to do with myself with the summer laid out before me. I have this nagging feeling that only one thing could ever bring us close to each other again.

Our friendship has always had its foundation in the thrill of danger and secrets. Even when we were little kids, it was always about sneaking around behind everyone's back. Skeleton Creek was full of rubes, and it was our job to pull one over on them.

It feels like those days are over.

Unless something happens.

Unless the thing that drove us apart is, in the end, the one thing powerful enough to bring me and Sarah back together.

Unless the ghost of Old Joe Bush returns.

I KNOW THAT SOUNDS CRAZY.

THE GHOST IS GONE. EVERYONE SAYS THE GHOST IS GONE.

BUT IF HE IS, WHY CAN I STILL FEEL HIS PRESENCE?

IF HE'S DISAPPEARED, HOW DO I KNOW HE'S STILL HERE?

MONDAY, JUNE 20, 9:45 A.M.

I SWEAR, THE WAITRESS JUST TRIED TO LOOK OVER MY SHOULDER.

I'M SO TIRED OF FEELING WATCHED.

ONE SECOND.

THE DREDGE STILL SITS OUT THERE IN THE WOODS, SAME AS IT EVER WAS, AND I NEVER GO OUT THERE. TOURISTS SEEM TO LIKE IT, WHICH IS WHAT PROMPTED MAYOR BLAKE TO PUSH THE IDEA OF A HAUNTED ATTRACTION. SORT OF LIKE A HAUNTED HOUSE. I THINK THIS IS A TERRIBLE IDEA, AND I'VE SAID AS MUCH. BUT WHO'S GOING TO LISTEN TO A SIXTEEN-YEAR-OLD, EVEN IF HE DID SAVE THE TOWN?

A FRESH CUP OF COFFEE AND I STILL HAVE A LITTLE TIME BEFORE I HAVE TO OPEN THE FLY SHOP. THAT SHOULD BE ENOUGH TIME TO ADDRESS THE MOST IMPORTANT THING I TOOK FROM THE DREDGE THAT NIGHT. IT WASN'T THE HORDES OF GOLD WE FOUND HIDDEN IN THE FLOORBOARDS, SECRETLY STASHED BY JOE BUSH LONG BEFORE HE WAS PULLED INTO THE GEARS AND DROWNED IN THE WATER BELOW. NO, IT WAS SOMETHING MUCH SMALLER AND INFINITELY MORE DANGEROUS.

THE LAST THING SARAH RECORDED IN THE DREDGE WAS A SHOT OF THE FLOOR. IF YOU LOOK AT THAT VIDEO, YOU'LL SEE THE SAME THING EVERYONE ELSE SAW: AN ENVELOPE. IT'S ONE OF THE GREAT MYSTERIES

OF THE DREDGE, AND ONE OF THE REASONS PEOPLE STILL THINK IT'S HAUNTED. BECAUSE YOU KNOW WHAT? NO ONE CAN FIND THAT ENVELOPE. IT'S AS IF IT NEVER EXISTED.

PEOPLE ASK ME ABOUT IT FROM TIME TO TIME. I JUST SHRUG AND SHAKE MY HEAD.

I DON'T FEEL LIKE LYING ANYMORE.

BUT I ALSO DON'T FEEL LIKE SAYING, "THE ENVELOPE? YEAH, I HAVE IT. I KEPT IT. HEY, SOMEONE'S GOTTA KEEP A LID ON THIS NIGHTMARE."

SO, YEAH, I TOOK THE ENVELOPE. IN ALL THE CONFUSION THAT NIGHT, I SLIPPED IT INTO MY POCKET AND DIDN'T TELL ANYONE, NOT EVEN SARAH. THEN I HID IT IN THE BACK OF ONE OF MY DESK DRAWERS AND TRIED TO FORGET. I THOUGHT MAYBE — JUST MAYBE — IF I DIDN'T ACKNOWLEDGE ITS EXISTENCE, IT WOULDN'T HAVE ANY POWER. IT WOULD SIT BACK THERE AND ROT LIKE AN OLD APPLE CORE.

BUT IT DIDN'T ROT. INSTEAD, IT BLOOMED IN MY IMAGINATION, AND A MONTH LATER I COULDN'T STAND LEAVING IT ALONE ANY LONGER. LIKE THE DISTANT, HOLLOW VOICE OF THE UNDEAD HIDDEN BENEATH OLD FLOORBOARDS, THIS GHASTLY THING WOULD NOT SHUT UP.

<u>WHAT'S INSIDE?</u> IT ASKED, SCRATCHING THE BACK OF MY BRAIN WITH ITS CLAWS.

I LAY THERE, NIGHT AFTER NIGHT, WONDERING WHAT HAD BEEN LEFT BEHIND, UNTIL FINALLY I COULDN'T STAND IT ANY LONGER.

A DISTANT THUNDER ROLLED OVER THE MOUNTAIN AT HALF PAST TWO IN THE MORNING AS I PULLED THE DRAWER ALL THE WAY OUT AND TOOK OUT THE DREADED ENVELOPE. RACING BACK TO MY BED, I FELT THE EVIL EYE OF OLD JOE BUSH WATCHING ME COWER BENEATH THE COVERS. WAS IT THE GHOST, OR WAS IT THE MAN, STANDING OUTSIDE MY WINDOW? I WOULD HAVE SWORN <u>SOMETHING</u> WAS THERE, TOUCHING THE GLASS AT MY SECOND—STORY WINDOW, AN ICY BREATH FOGGING THE PANE.

I TORE THE ENVELOPE OPEN AND HELD ITS CONTENTS IN MY HAND.

ONE CARD, TWO SIDES. THE WORK OF A MADMAN IF EVER THERE WAS!

SIDE ONE, WHICH I CAME TO CALL THE SKULL

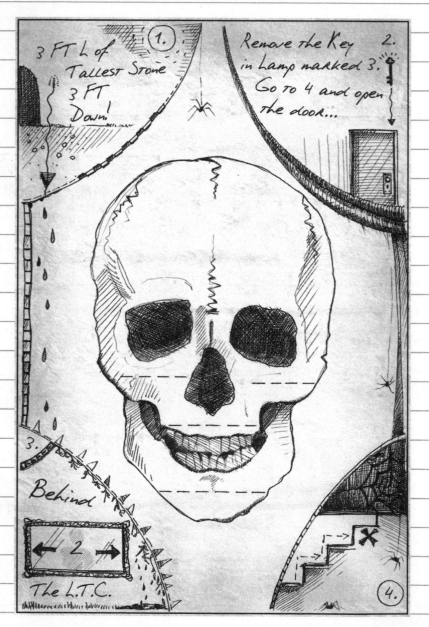

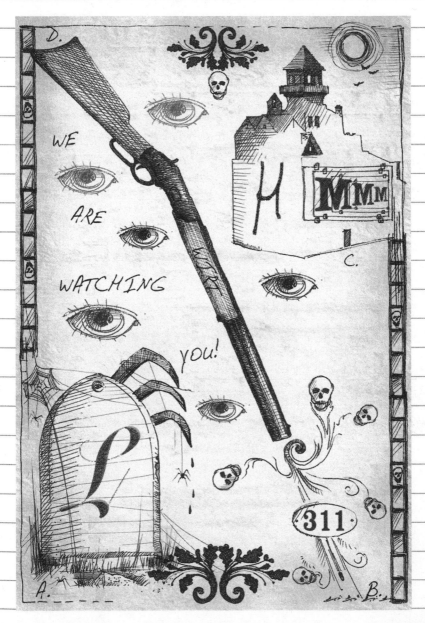

As a whole, I came to call this crazy thing I'd found the Skull Puzzle, because that's what it was: skulls and tombstones and guns. A puzzle of the dead.

I spent the next few months trying to figure out what the clues on the card meant. Many months, and a giant ZERO to show for my efforts. I searched online endlessly, all hours of the night, until I woke up one morning and realized the contents of the envelope had become my obsession.

I should have left the envelope at the back of my drawer, as I'd planned to do. Or better yet, I should have left it in the forsaken dredge where it belonged. Maybe the ghost of Old Joe Bush would have emerged from his watery grave and pulled it into the mud where it belonged.

But no. I had it now.

MONDAY, JUNE 20, 10:10 A.M.

There came a night when I decided to put it back. I had the feeling it was cursed, that it would send my mind spinning into oblivion if I kept it. Against all my better judgment, I took to the woods behind Skeleton Creek and made the long walk alone. But when I stood before the dredge in the dead of night, I was so scared I couldn't bring myself to go inside. I ran back through the woods, tree limbs slapping me in the face, and collapsed on my bed.

You have to understand: I almost died there.

It's hard to go back to a place where you almost died.

As I went to my laptop in search of some unattainable comfort, I knew deep in my bones that I would find a message from Sarah. I can't say why, other than to admit my belief that I am connected to Sarah in an otherworldly way. Say what you will, but I felt true terror at the dredge. The same panic Sarah felt on the night she first saw the ghost of Old Joe Bush. My fear, so closely linked to her own, called out to her.

I REALIZE EMAIL IS A DIGITAL INVENTION LACKING IN DRAMATIC REALITY, BUT THIS WAS ONE MESSAGE THAT PRODUCED FEELINGS I WILL NEVER FORGET.

Hi, Ryan,

I had a dream you were at the dredge without me and it made me sad. I miss you. I miss our secrets. There must be something we could do to get the magic back. But what?

S.

I EMAILED HER BACK IMMEDIATELY.

Sarah,

I can bring that feeling back. Tell no one, especially your parents.

R.

I attached the two images and had to wait only nine minutes for her reply. We spent the rest of that first night instant messaging, emailing web sites and images, whispering into our cell phones. By the time the sun came up, we'd spent five hours in constant communication.

Like the ghost of Old Joe Bush, we were back.

If only I'd known then what I know now, I never would have encouraged Sarah to go down this path with me. I never would have taken that envelope in the first place.

It was what they wanted, and we had it.

We didn't even know they were paying any attention.

The Crossbones were watching us.

We've made some progress, which I will explain after I get off work, but in the meantime, there's something to watch.

She's uploading videos again. Same web address, new passwords. It's different this time around, and I'm still getting used to it. Sarah never shows her face. I wish I could see her, but I understand why she's changed her recording methods. Nothing on the internet is safe, and videos get captured and posted all the time. She's much more comfortable behind the camera, not in front of it, but it's more than that.

Sarah is scared, just like I am.

She doesn't want the wrong people seeing her. She's even altered the way she sounds. It's <u>almost</u> her voice, but not quite. Kind of gives me the creeps, if you want to know the truth.

Sarah's first video is up there, a disturbing recap of everything that's happened so far to us. If I'm gone and you've stumbled onto this journal, maybe you need to see what happened

AT THE DREDGE. MAYBE YOU NEED AN INTRODUCTION TO THE CROSSBONES BECAUSE, LET ME TELL YOU, THEY MATTER. EVEN IF YOU ALREADY KNOW ABOUT THESE THINGS, HER TELLING IS WORTH A LOOK.

DON'T WATCH IT WITH THE LIGHTS OFF.

ALWAYS BE ON GUARD.

SARAHFINCHER.COM

PASSWORD:

MRSVEAL

As soon as I got that password from Sarah, I Googled it and found a digital copy of a short story called "A Relation of the Apparition of Mrs. Veal." Who knew Daniel Defoe, the same guy who wrote <u>Robinson Crusoe</u> (a fave of mine), also wrote a ghost story? "The Apparition of Mrs. Veal" is a short story about a lady who sees a woman wandering around on the day after her death. Not the most chilling thing I've ever read, but interesting in that it is said to have been taken from actual events.

I can relate.

Watching the entire story of what happened to us in three minutes is like seeing my life flash before my eyes. All those events happened over a period of only a few weeks, but looking back, it feels like a much bigger chunk of my life. I guess some memories are burned in forever while others blow away like leftover ash.

This version of events makes me feel something I haven't felt before:

What happened in the past was only the beginning.

Sarah and I have a ways to go before we're done.

I JUST SPENT THE DAY AT MY SUMMER JOB — A PRETTY GOOD GIG, ALL THINGS CONSIDERED.

MY PARENTS SAVED HALF OF THE MONEY THEY GOT FROM THE GOLD AND SUNK THE REST INTO A FLY SHOP, WHERE I AM GAINFULLY EMPLOYED AT A RATE WELL BELOW MINIMUM WAGE ALONG WITH ANOTHER YOUNG GUY NAMED SAM FITZSIMONS (EVERYONE CALLS HIM FITZ). MY DAD IS CONSTANTLY REMINDING ME THAT MY PAY IS WELL BELOW WHAT FITZ MAKES BECAUSE IT INCLUDES ROOM AND BOARD. THIS IS A TOTAL CROCK AND PROBABLY AGAINST THE LAW, BUT I'LL TAKE WHAT I CAN GET.

ACTUALLY, HIRING FITZ WAS MY IDEA. MY DAD MADE ME TRY OUT FOR THE FOOTBALL TEAM BACK IN OCTOBER AND I WAS CURSED TO MAKE THE C SQUAD. THE ONE GOOD THING THAT CAME OUT OF THE EXPERIENCE WAS FINDING A GUY WHO WAS JUST AS INEPT AT SPORTS AS I WAS. FITZ AND I RODE THE BENCH TOGETHER, TOOK HITS FROM THE A SQUAD AS PRACTICE DUMMIES, AND TALKED ABOUT FISHING THROUGH ENDLESS FRIDAY NIGHTS OF NO PLAYING TIME. WHEN FOOTBALL CAME TO AN END A COUPLE OF

MONTHS AGO, I STARTED PESTERING MY DAD TO HIRE THE GUY WHO'D SAT NEXT TO ME FOR THREE MONTHS OF WINTER GAMES.

"CAN HE TIE A FLY AND CAST A ROD?" WAS MY DAD'S ONLY QUESTION, WHICH I ANSWERED HUGELY IN THE AFFIRMATIVE. FITZ WAS A FISHING NUT, AND MY DAD WANTED CHEAP, EXPERIENCED, LOCAL LABOR. MY FOOTBALL BUDDY FIT THE BILL. FITZ WAS LIKE A LOT OF SIXTEEN-YEAR-OLD GUYS WHO LIVED IN THE MOUNTAINS: GOOD WITH A GUN, A FISHING ROD, AND A CAMPFIRE. AND CHEAPER THAN CHEAP TO EMPLOY, BECAUSE ALL HE REALLY WANTED TO DO WAS SPEND ALL HIS MONEY IN THE FLY SHOP, ANYWAY. A REAL WIN-WIN FOR MY DAD.

A LITTLE MORE ABOUT FITZ:

HE LIVES A FEW MILES OUTSIDE OF TOWN IN A TRAILER WITH HIS DAD — A SITUATION NOT AS UNCOMMON AROUND HERE AS ONE MIGHT IMAGINE. HIS DAD'S A LOGGER, WHICH IS MORE THAN LIKELY WHY HE'S DIVORCED. (LIFE LESSON: WOMEN DON'T DIG IMPOVERISHED WOODSMEN WHO SHOWER TWICE A WEEK.) FITZ RIDES AN OLD MOTORBIKE HELD TOGETHER BY DUCT TAPE AND CHICKEN WIRE AND NEVER WEARS A

HELMET. WE'RE A LITTLE SHY ON COPS AROUND HERE, AND EVEN IF WE HAD ANY, I DOUBT THEY'D CARE ABOUT TEENAGERS JOYRIDING IN THE BACK OF PICKUP TRUCKS OR RACING AROUND WITHOUT HELMETS ON. IT'S KIND OF PAR FOR THE COURSE IN SKELETON CREEK, IF YOU GET MY DRIFT.

FITZ'S MOTORCYCLE BURNS OIL, WHICH MEANS YOU CAN OFTEN SMELL HIM COMING BEFORE HE SHOWS UP. EVEN THOUGH I TELL HIM I DON'T MIND THE SMELL, HE WON'T LET ME RIDE IT. ONE OF THESE DAYS I'M GOING TO LIFT HIS KEYS AND DO COOKIES IN THE GRAVEL BEHIND THE FLY SHOP, BECAUSE, ACTUALLY, IT'S A SWEET BIKE. IT HAULS.

WHEN FITZ TALKS, IT'S ALMOST ALWAYS ABOUT FISHING AND HUNTING, WHICH IS A LITTLE WEIRD. THE ONLY BUMMER ABOUT HAVING HIM AROUND IS HE'S A VERY GOOD FISHERMAN AND AN EVEN BETTER FLY TIER. PLUS, HE'S A PEOPLE PERSON, UNLIKE ME. (GENERALLY SPEAKING, I PREFER NOT TO TALK WITH ANYONE I DON'T KNOW UNLESS I'M FORCED INTO IT.) I HAVE A HUNCH MY DAD IS GOING TO USE HIM A LOT TO TAKE TOURISTS FISHING AND LEAVE ME IN THE SHOP. IF THAT HAPPENS, I WILL HAVE TO KILL FITZ, BECAUSE I

CANNOT STAND THE IDEA OF FISHING STORIES IN WHICH I
AM NOT A PARTICIPANT.

I'M GOING DOWNSTAIRS FOR DINNER. THEN IT'S TIME
TO WRITE DOWN HOW ME AND SARAH ACCIDENTALLY
SUMMONED A GHOST AND A SECRET SOCIETY BACK INTO
OUR LIVES.

MONDAY, JUNE 20, 10:15 P.M.

I GOT ROPED INTO A FEW HOURS ON THE STREAM WITH FITZ AND MY DAD AFTER DINNER, BUT I'M FINALLY BACK. FITZ LANDED A MONSTER OUT OF THE BIG HOLE AT MILE 7, BUT IT WAS PRETTY SLOW OTHERWISE, AND I GOT SKUNKED. MY MIND WAS ON OTHER THINGS.

I WISH I COULD TELL FITZ WHAT'S GOING ON. I MEAN, WHAT'S REALLY GOING ON. BUT THAT'S NOT WHERE WE ARE RIGHT NOW. LIKE WITH MOST OF MY FRIENDS. I HAVE PLENTY OF PEOPLE I COULD HANG OUT WITH, OR PLAY VIDEO GAMES WITH, OR TALK ABOUT HOMEWORK WITH. BUT FRIENDS I CAN TELL EVERYTHING? JUST SARAH, AND EVEN HER, NOT REALLY. WHICH IS PROBABLY WHY I SPEND SO MUCH TIME WITH THESE NOTEBOOKS. IT'S EASIER THAN GETTING OTHER PEOPLE INVOLVED.

I NEED TO GO BACK AND RETRACE HOW I ENDED UP IN THE SITUATION I'M IN, BECAUSE REALLY, I DON'T KNOW EXACTLY HOW IT HAPPENED. IT'S BEEN THREE WEEKS SINCE I TOLD SARAH ABOUT THE SKULL PUZZLE. SHE CALLS IT THE SKULL. EITHER WAY, IT'S FULL OF SURPRISES.

"THE SKULL SAYS THIS AND THE SKULL SAYS THAT," SHE'LL TELL ME. OR "I THINK THIS IS WHAT THE SKULL IS TRYING TO TELL US."

Just like every other time before, she's got a way of taking the lead.

As I write this, Sarah is driving from Chicago.

Because of the Skull.

I know, crazy.

Here's how it happened, as best I can string it all together.

About a week after I sent Sarah the Skull Puzzle, she emailed me an idea that I hadn't thought of. I'd been looking at those images for months, feeling stumped by the weird collection of symbols and numbers. But Sarah's dad was a hunter and mine wasn't. Turns out that was the trigger that blew my whole life apart.

Hi, Ryan,

I've been thinking about the gun. That word on the barrel — Wirt — it's not what we thought. I looked up all the gun manufacturers again, and this time, I cross-checked owners and company owners. Ryan — it's not *Wirt*, it's *Winchester*. I kept focusing on the founder, Oliver

Winchester, but that was a dead end. But guess what his son's name was? William Wirt Winchester. So we know it's a Winchester gun! That's good, right?

Not much, but something.

S.

BY THE TIME I GOT THIS EMAIL FROM SARAH, I'D HAD THE SKULL FOR A LONG TIME. AT SOME POINT ALONG THE WAY I SCANNED IT AND TOOK IT APART, SEPARATING EACH ITEM INTO ITS OWN FILE.

HERE'S THE RIFLE AGAIN:

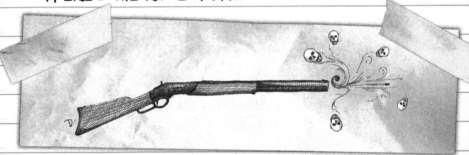

I DO NOT LIKE GUNS OF ANY KIND, AND THIS ONE IS NO EXCEPTION. I SEARCHED THE NAME WILLIAM WIRT WINCHESTER, AND BEFORE THE NIGHT WAS OVER, I KNEW WHAT I'D GOTTEN MY HANDS ON. SARAH AND I BOTH KNEW. THE EMAILS FLEW BACK AND FORTH AS WE MADE PROGRESS. IT WAS LIKE WE'D BEEN LOST IN THE WOODS AND HAD SUDDENLY FOUND THE RIGHT TRAIL.

Sarah,

Did you look up his name? If you do you'll find he was married to — get this — a lady named Sarah. That's crazy, right? And she was crazy. Her husband and her kid both died, and she had piles of money. She basically owned half the Winchester gun company during the Civil War. Can you imagine how many guns they sold? Hang on — I'm diving back in.

Ryan

Ryan,

The Winchester House in San Jose, California — freaky! I love it! I think it's even better than our own haunted dredge. Get this: Sarah (Winchester) started building the house after she got all that money and basically never stopped building. She believed that there had to be enough rooms to hold all the people who had ever been killed by a Winchester gun. Fat chance, Sarah — you'd need a house as big as Mexico for that. She came close! The Winchester House is gigantic and it's filled with doors that lead to nowhere, secret passageways, and lots of confirmed ghost sightings.

This is getting good.

S.

Sarah,

I got it. Check out this piece of the Skull Puzzle:

The part I blew up is marked with a number 4, which probably means it's a match for the letter D at the end of the gun:

The stairs don't make any sense. They end at the ceiling. The Winchester House is full of crazy stuff like this — you said so yourself. My guess? If we could figure out a way to find this exact spot in the house, we'd find one part of what we're looking for.

We could fill in one of the dotted lines on the Skull Puzzle and we'd be on our way to solving this thing.

R.

MONDAY, JUNE 20, 10:47 P.M.

IT'S GETTING LATE, BUT I DON'T CARE. I HAVE TO GET THIS ALL DOWN.

JUST IN CASE SOMETHING HAPPENS.

IT DIDN'T TAKE US LONG TO FIGURE OUT THAT WHAT I'D FOUND WAS A KEY TO A SERIES OF PLACES WHERE PARANORMAL ACTIVITY HAD BEEN RECORDED. SOMEONE HAD CREATED A HAUNTED TREASURE MAP . . . BUT WHERE DID IT LEAD AND WHAT WAS IT FOR? IN MY DARKEST THOUGHTS, I COULD ONLY IMAGINE ONE PLACE A MAP LIKE THAT WOULD TAKE ME, AND THAT WAS SIX FEET UNDERGROUND, WITH A TOMBSTONE OVER MY HEAD.

THIS WAS A MAP OF THE DEAD, MADE BY A GUY WHO'D LOST HIS MIND.

HENRY.

THERE, I SAID IT.

HENRY, WHO BETRAYED MY FAMILY, MY TOWN, AND ME. HENRY, WHO DISAPPEARED LIKE A GHOST. HENRY, THE TRAITOR. HENRY, THE THREAT.

THIS WAS HENRY'S DOING. THE SKULL PUZZLE CAME OUT OF HIS TWISTED MIND AND LANDED IN HIS POCKET.

But when did he make it — before or after he was taken over by the ghost of Old Joe Bush?

Looking at everything through a ghostly lens sharpened our search dramatically. During that same night, Sarah and I figured out one of the other clues on the Skull: the strange house with an H and three M's on it.

Before we applied the haunted filter, these images could have meant a million different things. The building could have been a House of Pancakes for all we knew. Or, more likely, House of the Dead or House on Haunted Hill. All we had was an H, a building, and a mirror reflecting the letter M over and over again. Sarah and I started thinking of it as the House

Ryan,

I got it I got it I got it! Sometimes YouTube isn't a total waste of time. I found a video while doing a search for haunted mirrors and BANG — I found it! I can hardly type this, I'm shaking so much. Just watch the video and then let's risk a call. It's 2:30 a.m. here, so your parents have to be asleep. Call me when you're done watching!!

S.

OF MIRRORS, WHICH GAVE US THE DIRECTION WE WERE LOOKING FOR.

SHE SENT A LINK THAT HAD SOME GUY GIVING A GUIDED TOUR OF A HOTEL CALLED THE DRISKILL. FIVE MINUTES IN, I KNEW SARAH WAS RIGHT. FIRST OFF, THE DRISKILL IS TOTALLY HAUNTED, PROBABLY THE MOST HAUNTED HOTEL IN AMERICA. THERE ARE DOZENS OF GHOST STORIES ABOUT THIS PLACE, AND ONE OF THEM HAS TO DO WITH MIRRORS. THERE ARE THESE GIANT ONES IN THIS ONE ROOM, ALL OF THEM MADE BY SOME RICH DUDE IN MEXICO FOR CARLOTA, HIS LADY FRIEND. AND HIS NAME? MAXIMILIAN — THAT'S MAX WITH AN M, JUST LIKE IN THE MIRROR ON THE DRAWING.

Now the spooky part: This tour guide was telling a story about what happens if you go up there to the Maximilian Room all by yourself and look straight into one of the mirrors. What it does is reflect to an identical mirror on the opposite wall. Then it reflects back again, so you basically look into a never-ending series of smaller and smaller mirrored images of yourself. And into that endless collection of you and only you walks Carlota! She just appears, out of nowhere, stares at you, and then you're dead. Okay, the dead part I made up, but you might die when you run screaming for your life, trip, and fall down the stairs.

The connecting image on the Skull Puzzle is this one:

Behind

2

The L.T.C.

This seemed pretty straightforward. There's an image of a person behind the two. It's soft, but it's there. Carlota! The rest also makes sense in the context of five mirrors on one wall. The two and the arrows mean there are two mirrors on either side, so that would make it one of the two middle mirrors. "Behind the L.T.C." has to mean "Behind the Left Top Corner."

Wow. We were getting pretty good at this puzzle stuff. The answers we were finding had to fill in the dotted lines in the Skull.

Four words, four haunted places — and we'd found two of them.

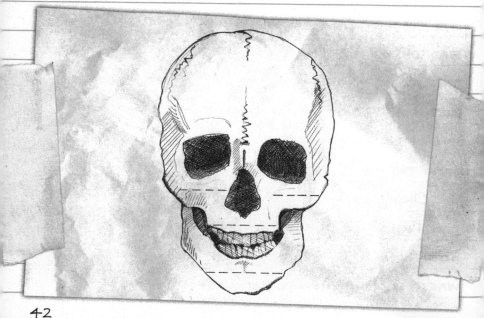

SORRY. HAD TO STOP THERE BECAUSE I HEARD DAD IN THE HALL.

I WISH I COULD TELL HIM ABOUT ALL THIS. BUT I KNOW I CAN'T.

HE WOULDN'T UNDERSTAND. HE'D TELL ME TO STOP. BOTH HIM AND MOM — THEY NEVER UNDERSTOOD WHAT SARAH AND I WERE UP TO. (OR MAYBE DAD KNEW ALL TOO WELL — BUT I DON'T WANT TO THINK ABOUT THAT.) THEY WERE GLAD WHEN SARAH LEFT. THEY THOUGHT IT MEANT I WOULD STOP DOING THINGS LIKE THIS — STAYING UP ALL NIGHT, DIGGING INTO PLACES I SHOULD LEAVE ALONE.

MOM AND DAD, IF YOU'RE THE FIRST PEOPLE WHO FIND THIS — IF SOMETHING'S HAPPENED — KNOW THAT THERE'S NO WAY YOU COULD HAVE STOPPED ME. IT'S NOT YOUR FAULT. I JUST HAVE TO DO THIS. IT DOESN'T EVEN FEEL LIKE A CHOICE. THE MYSTERY FOUND ME. AND THE ONLY WAY TO GET RID OF IT IS TO SOLVE IT.

OKAY, BACK TO THE SKULL PUZZLE. THE NEXT DAY I KNOCKED OFF THE THIRD OF THE FOUR LOCATIONS: THE HORNED TOMBSTONE WAS MINE. THIS WAS THE ONE IMAGE WE SHOULD HAVE FIGURED OUT

SOONER, BECAUSE WHAT SAYS <u>HAUNTED</u> MORE THAN A TOMBSTONE? BUT THERE ARE AN AWFUL LOT OF CEMETERIES OUT THERE FULL OF A LOT OF ZOMBIES AND GHOSTS, SO HOW WERE WE TO KNOW WHICH ONE THIS PARTICULAR TOMBSTONE REFERRED TO?

THERE WAS AN L ETCHED ON THE STONE, BUT THAT COULD MEAN A LOT OF THINGS. IT WAS MY MOM, BELIEVE IT OR NOT, WHO HELPED ME SOLVE THIS ONE.

I TOOK THE SCAN I HAD AND CAREFULLY CUT OUT THE L, NO HEADSTONE. I ALSO ISOLATED THE REPEATING HORN THAT STUCK OUT OF THE RIGHT SIDE. AFTER PRINTING THEM BOTH ON ONE PIECE OF PAPER, I WENT AND SAT ON THE PORCH WITH THE NOTEBOOK I WRITE MY STORIES IN.

Mom was sipping an iced tea with lemonade, otherwise known as an Arnold Palmer, the heat of summer dropping her to the old couch like a sack of potatoes. I opened my journal and set the piece of paper on the scuffed coffee table. Bingo. I'd opened up the world of my notebooks to my mom, a rare occurrence. She wasted no time asking me what I was working on.

"A ghost story," I said. This was the most common of answers, which is to say it gave my mom no information. She picked up the piece of paper and gave it a long once-over.

"A haunted farm?" she asked. "Please don't cut people up with the blades."

"The what?" I asked.

"The plow blades. Don't put them in the hands of a monster and cut people up. You're above that. I didn't raise a blood-spilling novelist."

I asked her to tell me what she was talking about, and a few seconds later I was good and educated about how a farmer plows a field. The repeating horns on the tombstone weren't horns at all — they were the blades of a plowshare,

45

THE KIND THAT GET PULLED BY A HORSE. OLD-SCHOOL, FOR SURE, BUT A DIRECTION I HADN'T TRIED.

IT DIDN'T TAKE ME LONG TO FIND MYSELF ONCE AGAIN EMAILING SARAH.

Sarah,

You're not going to believe this, but I figured out the horned tombstone. Those aren't horns! They're blades from a plow, and this tombstone is in a cemetery that's only a fifteen-hour drive from your front door!

It's called the Bachelor's Grove Cemetery, and it's a perfect match. There's a pond on the grounds and a farmer was pulled in there by his crazy plow horse. And guess what drove the plow horse nuts? A lady in white — the letter L — who wandered across the horse's path and sent it into a wild rage. The farmer haunts the place along with the lady and the horse, a triple threat, plus about a hundred other undead creatures of the night. It's a seriously bad place.

And guess where it is? Bachelor's Grove, Chicago. Like I said, fifteen hours from your front door. It's abandoned, so no one will be around. Unless you count the dead people.

Ryan

THE REALLY HORRIBLE PART ABOUT THE HORNED
TOMBSTONE WAS THE PART OF THE SKULL THAT
REFERRED TO WHERE THE CLUE WOULD BE HIDDEN.
SARAH POINTED THAT OUT IN HER NEXT EMAIL, WHICH
SHOWED UP ABOUT AN HOUR AFTER I SENT MINE.

R—

You do realize that even I'm not thrilled about digging three feet deep
in an abandoned cemetery, right? You may have finally found something
even I won't do.

S.

SHE WAS TALKING ABOUT THIS:

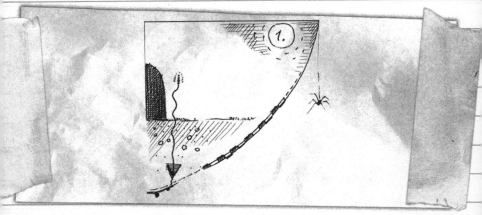

Not a fun message, even in broad daylight. Whatever this pointed to would need to be dug up in a cemetery. Totally verboten in Ryan's playbook, but it would need to be done.

Are there laws about stuff like this? I mean, could Sarah go to jail for digging up a cemetery? More important, could Sarah die from digging up a cemetery? I think that's possible. I was just glad she was far enough away from the rest of the places to make it impossible to track them all down.

At least that's what I thought until she told me the incredibly stupid plan she'd come up with.

This time, she called me, middle of the night, phone vibrating my brain awake from under my pillow.

"I called you six times," she started. "You are one heavy sleeper."

"Sorry. What's wrong?"

"Nothing's wrong. I just couldn't wait to tell you the good news."

"It's summer and it's four thirty in the morning," I reminded her.

"Not in Boston. Here it's seven thirty and I just ate oatmeal with my parents."

"And I care about this why?"

"Because they said yes. I guess turning seventeen opened a few doors for me."

I sat up in bed, because I knew what this yes she was talking about meant.

"You're not serious," I said.

"Oh, yeah, I'm serious. Haunted road trip."

I couldn't believe it. I mean, I REALLY couldn't believe it. Sarah and I had talked about it, but this was unbelievable. My parents wouldn't even

LET ME DRIVE DOWN THE HILL FOR A CHEESEBURGER WITHOUT MAKING SURE I HAD MY GPS PHONE ON RED ALERT SO THEY COULD TRACK MY EVERY MOVE. <u>MAN</u>, SARAH WAS LUCKY.

SARAH HAD WORKED IT TO THE HILT, TELLING HER PARENTS THAT IT WOULD BE THE BEST STUDENT PROJECT EVER IF SHE COULD DRIVE TO SUMMER FILM SCHOOL IN CALIFORNIA AND MAKE A DOCUMENTARY ALONG THE WAY. SHE WOULD STOP AT INTERESTING LOCATIONS, VISIT WITH DIFFERENT FAMILY MEMBERS COAST TO COAST, AND CREATE THE COOLEST VIDEO DIARY ANY FILM SCHOOL TEACHER HAD EVER SEEN. IT WAS GOING TO BE AMAZING.

"TURNS OUT I HAVE RELATIVES SPREAD OUT ALL OVER THE COUNTRY," SARAH TOLD ME. "I'M ONLY STAYING IN TWO HOTELS. THE REST IS AUNTS, UNCLES, AND MY PARENTS' OLD COLLEGE ROOMMATES. JUST DRIVE, EAT, FILM. OH, AND MAKE A FEW STRATEGIC STOPS ALONG THE WAY."

IT WASN'T EXACTLY A STRAIGHT SHOT, BUT IT WAS CLOSE. BOSTON TO CHICAGO, THEN AUSTIN, AND FINALLY CALIFORNIA: BACHELOR'S GROVE CEMETERY, THE DRISKILL HOTEL, THE WINCHESTER HOUSE.

"I'LL HAVE TO CUT SOME CORNERS HERE AND THERE TO STAY ON SCHEDULE, BUT I'VE GOT SEVEN DAYS TO GET ACROSS AMERICA BY CAR. THEY TOTALLY BOUGHT IT!"

THERE WAS ONLY ONE PROBLEM: WE DIDN'T KNOW WHERE THE LAST LOCATION WAS. THERE WERE FOUR THINGS TO FIND, AND WE'D ONLY FOUND THREE. THE MEANING OF THE NUMBER 311 CONTINUED TO ELUDE US, AND THE LONGER IT TOOK TO FIGURE OUT, THE MORE LIKELY SARAH WOULD HAVE TO BACKTRACK OR CHANGE COURSE.

"I'LL HANDLE THINGS ON THE ROAD," SHE TOLD ME. "YOU JUST FIND THAT LAST LOCATION BEFORE I END UP A THOUSAND MILES ON THE OTHER SIDE AND CAN'T

MAKE IT BACK IN TIME. REMEMBER, EVERY MILE IS DOUBLE IF I'M BACKTRACKING, AND THERE'S VERY LITTLE ROOM FOR ERROR. MY PARENTS WILL FREAK IF I DON'T SHOW UP ON TIME WHERE I'M SUPPOSED TO."

WHEN I HUNG UP THE PHONE, I WAS ONE PART JEALOUS, ONE PART EXCITED, AND FIVE PARTS SCARED OUT OF MY SHORTS.

WE WERE ABOUT TO UNLOCK A MESSAGE THAT WOULD LEAD TO TROUBLE OF THE WORST KIND. I WAS SURE ABOUT THIS, AND SO WAS SARAH. WE BOTH KNEW IT WAS A BAD IDEA, BUT WE COULDN'T HELP OURSELVES.

AND DO YOU WANT TO KNOW WHY WE KNEW IT WAS A BAD IDEA?

BECAUSE THE GHOST OF OLD JOE BUSH WAS WATCHING US. HE KNEW WHAT WE WERE UP TO.

WE KNEW THIS BECAUSE HE SENT US A MESSAGE YESTERDAY. A VIDEO. TO OUR PERSONAL EMAILS.

IT WASN'T GOOD.

IF YOU WANT TO SEE IT FOR YOURSELF, YOU CAN FIND IT AT SARAH'S SITE. BUT BE WARNED — IT'S NOT RIGHT. IT MIGHT KEEP YOU UP AT NIGHT.

SARAHFINCHER.COM
PASSWORD:
FACEINTHEMIRROR

TUESDAY, JUNE 21, 7:00 A.M.

You're hiding something, aren't you, Ryan McCray? Something of mine, maybe? Something I left behind. Don't be surprised if HE comes looking for you. I won't be able to stop him. Even I can't protect you from that one.

It will burn, burn, burn and you won't get it out.

The ghost of Old Joe Bush is back. Not Henry — some other version of him, and, man, is he not happy.

He will get you! — I think he is Henry, and the ghost of Old Joe Bush is trying to warn me, not the other way around.

Burn, burn, burn! I think he means that what's to come will be seared into my memory, never to fade away. Whatever wild ride I'm in for, I'll remember it when I'm ninety . . . as if I have any chance of living that long.

Riddles upon riddles — that's what you get when you're dealing with a lunatic wrapped in a ghost.

I realize I should tell someone about this. I really do. There's a madman out there sending

ME VIDEOS AND I'M NOT RUNNING TO MY PARENTS? IT'S HARD TO EXPLAIN, BUT I THINK WHAT'S GOING ON HERE IS VERY DEEP. I THINK I HAVE A CONNECTION TO OLD JOE BUSH THAT MAKES ME DO THINGS I WOULDN'T OTHERWISE IMAGINE ON MY OWN. ME AND JOE BUSH HAVE A LOT IN COMMON. BOTH OF US ARE (OR WERE) KNOWN FOR SNEAKING AROUND AND HIDING THINGS. I WANT MY LIFE TO BE EXCITING, BUT I'M STUCK IN SKELETON CREEK. I THINK JOE FELT THE SAME WAY. TRAPPED, PARANOID, FORCED TO KEEP SECRETS HE DIDN'T WANT TO BE IN CHARGE OF. IT MAKES ME WONDER IF I'LL BE A GHOST SOMEDAY, HAUNTING SOME OTHER KID IN SOME OTHER SMALL TOWN. IT SOUNDS A LITTLE BORING, IF YOU WANT THE TRUTH. DAYS AND NIGHTS FILLED WITH STANDING AROUND DOING ALMOST NOTHING. ANYWAY, THE POINT IS, I DON'T KNOW WHERE THIS IS ALL LEADING, BUT SOMETHING TELLS ME I SHOULD DO THINGS THE WAY I'VE ALWAYS DONE THEM: SECRETLY, AT LEAST UNTIL I KNOW WHAT'S REALLY GOING ON, AND WHO I CAN REALLY TRUST.

SARAH IS OFFICIALLY ON THE ROAD. I COULDN'T TALK HER OUT OF IT, AND TONIGHT SHE ARRIVES IN CHICAGO. SHE'LL HAVE TO VISIT THE CEMETERY

AFTER DARK, WHICH POSES CERTAIN PROBLEMS. SHE HAS AN AUNT AND UNCLE WHO LIVE ABOUT AN HOUR OUTSIDE OF THE CITY AND THEY'RE EXPECTING HER FOR DINNER. SHE'LL NEED TO SNEAK OUT OF THE HOUSE AFTER EVERYONE IS ASLEEP, DRIVE TWO HOURS TO THE CEMETERY, DIG UP WHATEVER IS HIDDEN THERE, AND GET BACK BEFORE DAWN.

THAT MEANS THE GRAVE DIGGING WILL ALMOST CERTAINLY HAPPEN AFTER MIDNIGHT, WHICH IS BASICALLY BEYOND MY ABILITY TO IMAGINE. ALONE IN AN ABANDONED CEMETERY AT NIGHT, DOING UNSPEAKABLE THINGS — IT DOESN'T GET ANY SCARIER THAN THAT, AND MY BEST FRIEND WILL BE DOING IT ALONE.

THAT IS, IF SHE DOESN'T GET CAUGHT SNEAKING OUT OF HER UNCLE'S HOUSE.

It's two or three in the afternoon wherever Sarah is, and she just texted me at work.

<u>Stopped for a late lunch</u>, 2 hours to go. <u>Waffle House!</u>

Living in the West, I have never experienced a Waffle House. It's Sarah's favorite fast-food restaurant because it serves breakfast all day and it's dirt cheap. She says the grits are to die for and the waffles are a crispy slice of heaven. Plus, the characters that hang out at the Waffle House tend to be chatty, older gentlemen with time on their hands. She doesn't outright talk to many of them, because she doesn't have to. They're generally on a first-name basis with the waitresses, and the conversations run thick.

This is how Sarah describes it:

"There's something right about hearing old memories from an old voice, the smell of waffles in the air while I sip my coffee. It's magic."

Actually, I think it's Sarah that's magic. Most people wouldn't see anything special about a place like that; they'd miss what really matters. But Sarah sees the loneliness and the longing and the two-dollar-and-fifty-cent comfort. She knows what to look for.

I used my lunch break to text back and forth with Sarah, something my dad strictly prohibits in the shop. He has a frightening aversion to text messaging in general.

"It's a phone," he has said more than once while I tap out a note on the tiny keyboard. "It's for making calls, not for writing novels."

I wouldn't say the world is passing my dad by, but he's easily two steps behind at all times. He has no patience for the things he sees no use for, so rather than endure his wrath, I take my break walking down Main Street while I hold a conversation with Sarah.

Sarah: Rest stops are gross.

Me: Please don't tell me more.

Sarah: I'm an hour from my uncle's house!

Me: Nervous about tonight?

Sarah: Got my grave digger in the trunk. A brand-new shovel. At least I have a weapon if I need it.

ME: MIGHT DO BETTER WITH A HAMMER. THE UNDEAD DON'T GO DOWN WITHOUT A FIGHT.

SARAH: IS THIS CONVERSATION SUPPOSED TO MAKE ME FEEL BETTER?

ME: JUST TAKE IT SLOW AND BE CAREFUL. NOTHING CRAZY. IF YOU SHOW UP AND IT DOESN'T FEEL RIGHT, GET THE HECK OUT OF THERE FAST.

WALKING AND TEXTING AT THE SAME TIME HAS A WAY OF PUTTING ME IN THE CROSSHAIRS OF SOMEONE I COULD HAVE AVOIDED IF I'D BEEN PAYING ATTENTION. WHEN I LOOKED UP FROM THAT LAST TEXT, WHICH TOOK QUITE A WHILE TO TAP OUT, I WAS FACE-TO-FACE WITH GLADYS MORGAN, THE TOWN LIBRARIAN. IF YOU ARE FAMILIAR WITH GLADYS, THEN YOU KNOW HOW SCARY THIS WOMAN CAN BE. SHE'S TALL AND BIG-BONED, WHICH MATCHES HER TOWERING PERSONALITY. A SMILE ALMOST NEVER APPEARS ON HER WRINKLED FACE.

"THAT'S THE DUMBEST INVENTION IN THE HISTORY OF DUMB IDEAS," SHE INFORMED ME. "BE CAREFUL YOU DON'T WALK INTO THE STREET. YOU'RE LIKELY TO GET RUN OVER BY A TOURIST DOING THE SAME THING BEHIND THE WHEEL OF A CAR."

"Thanks, Miss Morgan. I'll keep that in mind."

"Don't patronize me, Mr. McCray. It will come back to haunt you."

Sitting on the bench outside the library, writing all this down, I realize that a Waffle House in Minnesota would be a great place to drop Gladys Morgan and forget to pick her up. Let her bug someone else for a change.

TUESDAY, JUNE 21, 2:12 P.M.

SOME GUY JUST CALLED THE SHOP ON HIS WAY INTO TOWN WITH THREE BUDDIES AFTER HEARING THE EVENING HATCH WAS ON. THEY WANT GUIDES FOR THE BIG RIVER AN HOUR TO THE EAST. FOUR CUSTOMERS MEANS TWO RAFTS AND TWO GUIDES, AND MY DAD JUST CHOSE ME OVER FITZ.

THIS PRESENTS A SERIOUS MORAL DILEMMA FOR ME. IF I BACK OUT, THEN FITZ GETS THE GIG AND I'M STUCK IN THE SHOP ALL NIGHT. UNDER NORMAL CIRCUMSTANCES, THIS WOULD BE A CATASTROPHE. I LIKE FITZ, BUT THERE'S NO DOUBT WE'RE IN A SUMMER-LONG COMPETITION FOR GUIDING GIGS. IT'S FIFTY BUCKS A POP PLUS TIPS AND IT'S TIME ON THE WATER. I'VE BEEN FLY-FISHING MY WHOLE LIFE, AND THE WATER HAS A CERTAIN PULL THAT CAN'T BE EXPLAINED. SAYING NO TO AN EVENING HATCH WITH BIG TROUT SIPPING THE SURFACE IS VERY NEARLY BEYOND MY COMPREHENSION. ESPECIALLY GIVEN THE FACT THAT PUTTING FITZ ON A BOAT WHEN I WAS ASKED FIRST SENDS A CERTAIN MESSAGE TO MY DAD. THIS COULD BECOME AN UNWELCOME PATTERN PRETTY FAST. I

COULD BE SITTING IN THE SHOP ALL SUMMER LONG WATCHING THE CLOCK TICK WHILE FITZ IS OUT EARNING A LOT MORE MONEY AND HAVING THE TIME OF HIS LIFE.

STILL, IT WAS NO CONTEST. THERE WAS NO WAY I COULD LET SARAH SHOW UP AT A CEMETERY WITHOUT HAVING ME ON THE PHONE TO KEEP HER CALM.

SO I TOLD MY DAD I HAD A STOMACHACHE, A HEADACHE, AND I'D JUST THROWN UP IN THE BATHROOM.

"IT'S JUST NERVES. YOU'LL BE FINE," WAS HIS ANSWER.

FITZ WAS VISIBLY BUMMED OUT. HE WANTED THIS GIG AS BAD, OR WORSE THAN I DID, SO I TOLD MY DAD I'D BE HAPPY TO LET FITZ HAVE THE FIRST GO OF THE SUMMER AND TAKE THE NEXT RUN. UNFORTUNATELY FOR ME, MY DAD WOULD NOT BUDGE. I COULD SEE IT IN HIS EYES. HE WAS TAKING HIS OWN KID OUT ON THIS ONE WHETHER I LIKED IT OR NOT, AND THAT WAS FINAL.

MY ONLY OTHER OPTION WAS TO FALL DOWN OUTSIDE AND BREAK MY ARM OR STICK A FLY HOOK IN MY FOREHEAD, AND I WASN'T EVEN SURE THOSE OPTIONS WOULD TIE ME DOWN IN THE SHOP FOR THE EVENING. NOPE, I'LL BE LOADING A BOAT OFF THE WATER AT

DARK ON A RIVER WITH NO CELL SERVICE AT 9:00, AND I WON'T BE BACK IN A PLACE WHERE I CAN CONTACT SARAH UNTIL AT LEAST 10:30.

WHICH IS 12:30 A.M., SARAH'S TIME.

I TRIED TEXTING SARAH, BUT SHE WOULDN'T TEXT BACK. THEN I CALLED, BUT SHE DIDN'T PICK UP. I COULDN'T DO ANYTHING BUT LEAVE HER A VOICE MESSAGE.

I GOT ROPED INTO A RIVER RUN — TRIED TO GET OUT OF IT BUT COULDN'T — PLEASE FORGIVE ME. I'LL TEXT YOU THE SECOND I GET BACK. BE CAREFUL!

SARAH WAS GOING TO HAVE TO DO THIS ALONE, JUST LIKE WHEN THIS WHOLE NIGHTMARE STARTED.

I HOPE SHE DOESN'T DRIVE OVER HERE AND HIT ME WITH HER SHOVEL.

WEDNESDAY, JUNE 22, 1:00 A.M.

BEST NIGHT OF FISHING EVER. NORMALLY, I'D BE ECSTATIC ABOUT CATCHING TWO DOZEN LUNKERS IN ONE TRIP, BUT TONIGHT, IT WAS AGONIZING. THE BETTER THE FISHING GOT, THE LONGER I KNEW WE'D STAY ON THE RIVER. EVEN AFTER I PULLED THE RAFT TO THE SHORE AT DARK, DAD LET THEM FISH FOR ANOTHER FORTY MINUTES. I KEPT CHECKING MY PHONE — NO SERVICE! — PRACTICALLY PULLING MY HAIR OUT WITH FRUSTRATION. I'M FINALLY GETTING A CHANCE TO PUT THE NIGHT'S EVENTS ON PAPER, BUT I'M SO TIRED FROM WORK I CAN HARDLY KEEP MY EYES OPEN. ROWING FOR FIVE HOURS TAKES A LOT OUT OF A GUY, BUT I HAVE TO WRITE THIS DOWN WHILE IT'S FRESH IN MY HEAD.

FIRST THINGS FIRST: MY DAD IS ONTO US. I MESSED THAT UP BIG-TIME.

"IF YOU'RE TRYING TO REACH SARAH, YOU CAN FORGET IT," HE SAID AFTER THE THIRD TIME HE CAUGHT ME CHECKING FOR CELL SERVICE.

WHEN HE CAUGHT ME A FOURTH TIME, HE SAID, "THIS IS THE LAST TIME YOU BRING THAT THING. DO YOUR JOB."

But the fifth time was the kicker. He didn't have to say anything, because the look on his face told me everything I needed to know. It was the same look he gave me when I was getting into real trouble with Sarah last year. It's a very specific look — not impatience or frustration, but something far worse: distrust. He's only ever looked at me that way when it involved Sarah. He knew we were back in serious contact, and he suspected we were doing something that might get us killed.

Later, when we were alone at the shop and were putting away the rafts and the gear, he came up next to me in the dark and gave me a real earful.

"I'm not going to be happy if you and Sarah are up to your old tricks again. Don't do anything stupid."

I covered as best I could, but I knew he was only one phone call away from talking to Sarah's dad and discovering she was on her way

TO CALIFORNIA. HE'D SMELL TROUBLE AT THAT POINT, NO DOUBT, BUT THERE WAS NOTHING I COULD DO TO STOP HIM.

THANKFULLY, DAD WAS EVEN MORE TIRED THAN I WAS WHEN WE FINALLY ARRIVED BACK AT THE HOUSE AT 10:45. WE FOUND A NOTE FROM MOM, AND TWO PLATES OF FRIED CHICKEN AND COLESLAW IN THE FRIDGE. I TOOK MINE UPSTAIRS TO MY ROOM SO I COULD FINALLY BE ALONE.

I LOOKED AT MY PHONE LIKE IT MIGHT REACH OUT AND TRY TO STRANGLE ME WITH GUILT, WHICH IS BASICALLY WHAT HAPPENED.

SEVEN TEXT MESSAGES, THREE CALLS, ONE VOICE MAIL. ALL OF THEM MISSED, ALL OF THEM FROM SARAH.

FIRST, THE AWFUL STRING OF TEXT MESSAGES:

9:47 P.M.
I'M HERE! DROP ME A TEXT, LET ME KNOW YOU'RE ALONE. I WANT YOU ON THE PHONE SO YOU CAN HEAR ME SCREAMING.

9:52 P.M.

WHERE ARE U?????????? No WAY YOU'RE STILL ON THE RIVER.

9:58 P.M.

SERIOUSLY, RYAN. THIS ISN'T FUNNY. CALL ME. IT'S CRAZY DARK OUT HERE.

10:10 A.M.

TRIED CALLING TWICE. I'M AT THE END OF A DIRT ROAD. HEADLIGHTS ON TOMBSTONES. I DON'T THINK I CAN DO THIS.

10:14 A.M.

I CAN DO THIS.

10:21 A.M.

I'M GOING IN, YOU BIG CHICKEN!!!!

10:24 A.M.

ABOUT TO GET REALLY DIRTY. CAN'T TYPE WITH MUDDY FINGERS. IF MY PHONE RINGS NOW, I WILL JUMP OUT OF MY SHOES. DON'T CALL.

I HAVE NEVER FELT AS HELPLESS, LAME, AND GUILTY AS I DID READING THOSE MESSAGES, UNLESS YOU COUNT THE VOICE MAIL FROM SARAH:

"WHY DOES THIS FEEL FAMILIAR? BECAUSE YOU DID THE SAME THING AT THE DREDGE LAST YEAR! DO YOU HAVE ANY IDEA HOW SCARY IT IS STANDING ALONE IN AN ABANDONED CEMETERY AT MIDNIGHT WITH A SHOVEL IN YOUR HAND? NO, I GUESS YOU DON'T, SINCE YOU BAILED ON ME!

"DOESN'T MATTER — I GOT WHAT WE CAME FOR. I SHOULD BE BACK AT MY UNCLE'S PLACE BY 2:30 A.M., GRAB A FEW HOURS OF SLEEP, THEN I'LL CONVERT THIS THING. I'M NOT EVEN GOING TO TELL YOU WHAT IT IS. THAT'S THE PRICE YOU PAY FOR FISHING WHILE I'M DIGGING UP A GRAVE SITE. SWEET DREAMS. AT LEAST I'M ALIVE!

"OH, AND YES, THAT WAS THE CREEPIEST THING I'VE EVER DONE IN MY LIFE."

WOW. COULD I FEEL ANY WORSE? I DON'T THINK SO. IT'S A LITTLE OVER THE TOP THROWING IN THAT "DIGGING UP A GRAVE SITE" COMMENT, BECAUSE THAT'S

NOT WHAT SHE HAD TO DO. DID SHE? I'M PRETTY SURE SHE ONLY HAD TO DIG A HOLE AT A CEMETERY. THAT'S NOWHERE NEAR AS SCARY AS UNEARTHING AN ACTUAL GRAVE. I'M ALMOST SURE I WOULD HAVE BEEN FINE DIGGING A HOLE. I WOULD HAVE PRETENDED IT WAS MY BACKYARD.

THE COMBINATION OF A HYPERACTIVE GUILT COMPLEX AND NOT KNOWING WHAT SHE'D DUG UP WAS KILLING ME. WHAT IF IT WAS AN ARM BONE OR A SKULL OR MORE GOLD?

IT COULD BE ANYTHING.

BUT I DIDN'T HAVE THE GUTS TO CALL HER, KNOWING THAT SHE'D BE DRIVING, AND TIRED DRIVER + MIDDLE OF THE NIGHT + ANSWERING CELL PHONE = TROUBLE. IT'S BAD ENOUGH I'VE LET HER DOWN, SO IT'S BEST I DON'T CONTRIBUTE TO HAVING HER SWERVE OFF THE ROAD ON HER WAY BACK TO CHICAGO.

I TEXTED HER ONCE, BUT THAT WAS IT.

I'M SO SORRY. THE HATCH WAS ON AND MY DAD WOULDN'T CALL IT A NIGHT. I WAS STUCK!

SHE STILL HASN'T TEXTED ME BACK OR CALLED ME.

Maybe she's asleep.

Or maybe she got caught.

I wish I could be sure.

If I know Sarah, she'll be ringing my cell on her time zone, not mine, which means I'll probably hear from her by 5:00 a.m.

It's one call I know better than to miss.

WEDNESDAY, JUNE 22, 4:23 A.M.

THAT WAS CRUEL, EVEN AFTER I MISSED THE GRAVE-
DIGGING EVENT. SARAH CALLED ME AT 4:13 A.M. AND
WOKE ME OUT OF A DEAD SLEEP. NOTE TO SELF: DO
NOT EAT FRIED CHICKEN AT 11:00 P.M. AND NEGLECT
TO BRUSH TEETH. TOTALLY GROSS.

SARAH HADN'T GONE TO SLEEP LIKE SHE SAID SHE
WAS GOING TO. THAT GIRL IS WIRED AFTER MIDNIGHT —
SHE CAN KEEP GOING, AND GOING, AND GOING. I'VE
COME TO REALIZE THAT HER FAVORITE TIME TO EDIT
VIDEO IS THE MIDDLE OF THE NIGHT, WHEN EVERYONE
ELSE IS DREAMING (OR, IN MY CASE, HAVING
NIGHTMARES). AFTER SNEAKING BACK INTO HER UNCLE'S
GUEST ROOM AROUND 3:00 A.M. HER TIME, SHE WENT
STRAIGHT TO WORK ON A VIDEO THAT CONTAINS
FOOTAGE I NEVER WOULD HAVE EXPECTED.

THE FIRST HALF OF THE VIDEO IS CLEARLY
SOMETHING SHE'D BEEN WORKING ON FOR A WHILE. I
THINK SHE MAY ACTUALLY BE PLANNING TO USE THIS
TRIP AS A DOCUMENTARY FILM PROJECT FOR REAL,
BECAUSE THE FIRST PART IS THE HISTORY OF THE
CEMETERY, COMPLETE WITH GHOSTLY SIGHTINGS.
AFTER THAT, SHE INCLUDES HER OWN EXPERIENCE

DIGGING IN THE DIRT. WATCHING IT, MY GUILT CAME RUSHING BACK FULL FORCE.

But the most interesting part of the video?

The reveal of what she found. In some ways, it makes total sense. I should have seen it coming.

There was a box.

And inside that box?

Our first clue that the Crossbones are a lot more dangerous then we'd thought.

The Apostle is back . . . and spookier than ever.

This you GOTTA see.

SARAHFINCHER.COM
PASSWORD:
THELADYINWHITE

WEDNESDAY, JUNE 22, 8:42 A.M.

I have to hand it to Sarah — she's getting really good at making these videos. Back in the days of the dredge, her videos were still straight-up home-movie quality, but this was different. This was the first time I thought, holy cow, Sarah could actually be a Hollywood filmmaker someday. If I didn't know better, I would have said the documentary footage of the cemetery was real. It sure gave me the chills. But that was nothing compared to seeing the A-postle again. That guy always made my skin crawl. Seeing him again and realizing what his role in the Crossbones was only served to heighten my dread.

I now know three things I didn't know before:

— Sometime in the past, the A-postle's primary role was to document the history of the Crossbones. For whatever reason, he broke this description into different parts and hid the truth in various locations of his own choosing.

— The Crossbones is old. It was originally comprised of "super-patriots" who became concerned that America's experiment in democracy was in danger from the beginning.

— They had a three-part mission:

1) preserve freedom
2) maintain secrecy
3) destroy all enemies.

Troubling new information, for sure, and a load of new questions:

— Was the Apostle a lot more important than I originally gave him credit for?

— Was there something more to his death than what Sarah and I uncovered?

— What had the Apostle been doing in Skeleton Creek?

— What secrets did the Crossbones keep and what enemies did they destroy?

— And, possibly of greatest importance, what does my dad have to do with all of this? He's got the birdie tattooed on his arm, just like the Apostle has on his hand. Sarah made sure to point that out in her own clever but twisted way. My dad was in the Crossbones. Is he still?

Sarah is back on the road, heading for her next haunted tour stop, and I still haven't had any luck figuring out the last location she has to visit. This, I'm afraid, is a big problem.

She'll be in St. Louis by noon, Memphis by 5:00 p.m., and she's due in Little Rock, Arkansas, before dark. Her mom's college roommate lives there, and Sarah is hoping to put in some time at the Bill Clinton Library as part of her video project for camp. The faster she moves, the more likely we're never going to figure out what the number 311 stands for.

I PUT ON SOME PINK FLOYD AND LIE IN BED,
STARING AT THE CLUES.

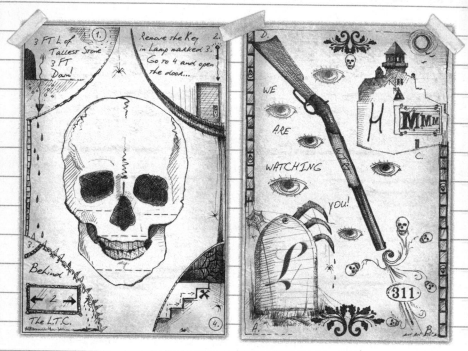

I THINK ABOUT THE CROSSBONES' THREE-PART MISSION:
1) PRESERVE FREEDOM 2) MAINTAIN SECRECY
3) DESTROY ALL ENEMIES.

ME AND SARAH FIT A LITTLE TOO COMFORTABLY
INTO NUMBER THREE.

DESTROY ALL ENEMIES.

THE MESSAGE IS CRYSTAL CLEAR: WE'RE A
THREAT TO THE CROSSBONES, SO THEY HAVE TO GET
RID OF US. IT FEELS LIKE SARAH'S TAKEN A BASEBALL

BAT TO A HORNETS' NEST AND NOW SHE HAS TO KEEP
MOVING, OUTRUNNING THE SWARM AS SHE HEADS WEST.

THE BOX SARAH DUG UP WAS BIG AND HEAVY. I'M
ACTUALLY SURPRISED SHE WAS ABLE TO GET IT OUT OF
THE GROUND BY HERSELF, NOW THAT I UNDERSTAND
WHAT WAS INSIDE: AN OLD-STYLE 8MM FILM
PROJECTOR AND A REEL OF FOOTAGE. SHE'D POINTED
THE PROJECTOR ON A WHITE WALL AND USED HER OWN
CAMERA TO CAPTURE THE IMAGE TO GET IT ONTO HER
COMPUTER — NOT THE MOST HIGH-TECH METHOD, BUT
IT HAD WORKED JUST FINE.

MY GUESS? THE REST OF THE LOCATIONS WILL
HAVE MORE REELS OF FILM, BUT NO PROJECTOR.

WE HAVEN'T HEARD THE LAST OF THE APOSTLE.

MY DAD JUST CHOSE FITZ TO GUIDE THE RIVER TODAY.

"NO NEED TO WORRY ABOUT ME, MR. McCRAY,"
FITZ SAID. "I DON'T EVEN <u>HAVE</u> A CELL PHONE."

<u>DUDE</u>, I WANTED TO SAY. <u>REMEMBER WHO
RECOMMENDED YOU FOR THE JOB?</u>

IN FAIRNESS, ONCE MY DAD WAS OUT OF THE ROOM,
FITZ TURNED TO ME AND SAID, "SORRY ABOUT THAT.
BUT YOU KNOW HOW IT IS WHEN YOU'RE STUCK IN THE
SHOP AND THE FISH ARE BITING. IT'S ROUGH."

THIS, I REMEMBERED, WAS WHAT FITZ AND I HAD IN
COMMON. IT WASN'T HIS FAULT MY DAD COULD ONLY
TAKE ONE OF US. HAD WE BEEN ABLE TO GO OUT, ALL
THREE, IT WOULD HAVE BEEN FANTASTIC, BECAUSE WE
ALL KNEW THE WATER BETTER THAN WE KNEW MOST
THINGS ON LAND.

"IT WAS PRETTY AWESOME," I ADMITTED, WITHOUT
TELLING HIM WHY I'D BEEN SO DISTRACTED.

UNDER NORMAL CIRCUMSTANCES, I WOULD HAVE
BEEN JEALOUS OF FITZ FOR GETTING TIME ON THE
RIVER WHILE I WAS GOING TO BE SITTING BORED IN
THE FLY SHOP ALL AFTERNOON. BUT IF TODAY IS
ANYTHING LIKE YESTERDAY, THEY'LL BE OUT UNTIL

LATE. AN EMPTY SHOP AND AN INTERNET CONNECTION IS EXACTLY WHAT I'VE BEEN HOPING FOR. STILL, MY DAD DIDN'T HAVE TO TELL FITZ I'D CONSTANTLY CHECKED MY PHONE YESTERDAY. THAT WAS HITTING BELOW THE BELT.

"BEST FISHING OF THE YEAR AND YOU'RE STUCK IN THE SHOP," FITZ SAID AS HE LOADED BOXES OF FLIES. "BEEN THERE, DONE THAT!"

OKAY, THAT HURT. BUT TURNABOUT WAS FAIR PLAY. I COULD ALREADY SEE HOW THE SUMMER WAS GOING TO GO. MY DAD WOULD PLAY ME AND FITZ AGAINST EACH OTHER ON EVERY FRONT. HOW MANY FISH DID YOU CATCH? HOW MANY FLIES DID YOU TIE? UNFORTUNATELY FOR ME, WHILE I'M FITZ'S EQUAL ON THE FOOTBALL FIELD (WE ARE BOTH PATHETIC LOSERS), HE IS THE BETTER FISHERMAN. I LOVE FISHING, BUT I DON'T LIVE IT. FITZ IS MORE IN THE MOLD OF MY DAD: THERE'S FISHING, AND THEN THERE'S EVERYTHING ELSE. THEY'RE BOTH AT A WHOLE DIFFERENT LEVEL OF ENTHUSIASM.

I'VE ALWAYS WONDERED WHAT IT WOULD BE LIKE TO HAVE A BROTHER. YOU CAN'T BE AN ONLY CHILD WITHOUT WONDERING. IMAGINE THAT — ANOTHER

McCray in the house. It wouldn't even matter if it was an older brother or a younger brother. There'd still be that competition.

I helped them pack up the supplies, and my mom stopped by with a cooler full of sandwiches, cans of soda, and homemade chocolate chip cookies.

"Looks good, Mrs. McCray," Fitz commented as he peered into the cooler. "You sure make a mean lunch."

Give it a rest, I thought.

"I brought you a sack of the same," my mom then said, handing me a white paper bag with a lunch in it. "See you for dinner?"

"Not likely," Dad answered for me. "If this is anything like last night, it'll be cold chicken and slaw again. We'll be out until at least an hour after dark, and I want Ryan here to help us unload."

Here again, I think my dad thought this was something of a punishment, when really he had given me free rein of the shop to help Sarah. This was going to be perfect.

Or at least that's what I thought. Then he gave me a piece of paper with a list of flies he wanted tied before he got back. If you've never seen or tied a fly for fishing, let me tell you, making them is no picnic. You start with a blank hook and a table full of material — feathers, fur, string, glue — seriously, like a million options, all so you can make what essentially amounts to a fancy fishing lure. My dad had just given me a whopper of an order for a whole slew of these things:

— 2 dozen gold-ribbed hare's ears, size 10 and 12 mixed
— 3 dozen orange stimulators, size 14
— 1 dozen woolly specials, number 8
— 2 dozen purple parachute adams, size 12

This was, no doubt, another reminder of how I just wasn't cutting it in the shop. Fitz was a known fly-tying machine. Eight dozen flies, which represented about two hundred dollars for the shop in sales, was nothing for Fitz.

"I can bang out a couple dozen before we leave if you want," Fitz told my dad.

Now he'd done it — he'd gone too far. I was smoldering with resentment, mostly because I knew he could whip together a dozen perfect flies a lot faster than I could tie six crappy ones.

"He's got all day and half the night," my dad said. "And no cell phone to distract him."

Uh-oh. This was bad. Dad held out his hand expectantly. Mom made a beeline for the door, because she knew I'd try to pit my parents against each other. She was gone before I could yell, "Mom, come on, tell him! How am I going to call you when I need a diaper change?"

I gave my dad my most seething look and removed the battery from my phone, handing him the rest. He turned away, mumbling something about how we were past all that. Fitz gave me a hopeless shrug, like he knew better: No matter how much parents tell you they won't read your texts, they will. It's written into the laws of parental physics. They can't help themselves, even if they did say they wouldn't do it.

84

After they took off, I felt a little better about one thing: My dad clearly hadn't called Sarah's dad yet. If he had, he would have mentioned it. No way could he know Sarah was on the road all by herself without saying something to me. Actually, this added up. When the hatch was on at the river, my dad was like a trout zombie: fish, eat, sleep, repeat. His mind was totally gone.

The shop was quiet and I had ninety-six flies to tie, which was a colossal enterprise for a guy Fitz likes to call "fumble fingers." He's totally right. He can tie about a dozen flies an hour, especially the easy ones, which is all my dad gave me (another not-so-subtle message about my lack of skill in this department). The list I got was like fly-tying 101 for beginners, but I'd be lucky to get in eight an hour, which meant if I didn't stop to use the bathroom or eat a cookie, I'd still be at it when they returned after dark.

So I started tying flies while several unanswerable questions ran through my head.

— What the heck does 311 mean?

— How angry is Sarah going to be when she finds out I've gone dark again?

— How in the world am I ever going to tie ninety-six flies without falling asleep?

WEDNESDAY, JUNE 22, 3:00 P.M.

Four hours, one sandwich, and thirty-seven flies. Not bad! I feel I'm slightly ahead of schedule and I have an idea about the number 311. I can't call Sarah from the shop phone because I know my dad will check the call list when he gets back in. We don't even <u>have</u> a home phone anymore, just cell phones in our pockets, so that's a bust. This leaves me at a bit of an impasse when it comes to reaching Sarah, who is surely almost to Memphis by now.

I'm closing the shop and walking down the street.

I think Gladys Morgan might be able to help me with the numbers. She's been around here forever and a day, since the time when the A-postle walked up and down the sidewalks all day trying to convert people. If anyone around here would know what the A-postle had been up to, it would be old Gladys.

I'VE JUST SPENT MORE THAN AN HOUR NOT TYING FLIES, WHICH PUTS ME WAY BEHIND SCHEDULE, BUT IT WAS TOTALLY WORTH IT.

I FIGURED OUT WHAT 311 MEANS. OR, MORE ACCURATELY, GLADYS MORGAN FIGURED IT OUT FOR ME. THIS IS HUGE — IT MEANS WE HAVE ALL FOUR LOCATIONS. IT MEANS THERE'S A CHANCE WE MIGHT ACTUALLY BE ABLE TO SOLVE WHATEVER THIS CRAZY THING IS.

THE NUMBER 311, SHOT VIOLENTLY OUT OF THE WINCHESTER LIKE A BULLET ON THE BATTLEFIELD. IT COULD HAVE MEANT SO MANY THINGS. FOR ALL I KNEW, IT WAS SOMEHOW ATTACHED TO THE WINCHESTER.

Old wrinkly Gladys steered me straight on that in a hurry once I got to the dusty library and started peppering her with questions. I had to handle it carefully, because like my dad, she had been part of the Crossbones. Who knew what she'd do if she found out I was digging up Crossbones history?

"So, Miss Morgan, have you ever thought of the number three-one-one in a spooky sort of way?" I asked her.

"You're a mixed-up child," she began. "Shouldn't you be minding the shop?"

"It's a slow day. I just needed a break."

"And you come down here to bother me? What are you up to?"

"I'm not up to anything. I'm just bored is all."

"I highly doubt that."

She sat there stewing for a good twenty seconds before saying another word, and even then, it wasn't an answer.

"Numbers can be deceiving."

"What's that supposed to mean?" I asked.

No reply, so I switched tactics.

"Did you know the A-postle back in the day? The preacher up the road said the A-postle knew something about what the numbers meant."

A huge lie — and about a preacher, no less. I felt my toes getting warm, like I'd sunk one level closer to a lake of fire.

Gladys was as old as the dredge. If anyone knew about the A-postle it would be her.

"Sure, I knew the A-postle. A highly annoying little man, if you ask me. He was always yelling at everyone he met."

"I don't understand."

And then she looked at me real funny, like she was trying to see inside my head.

"He preached fire and brimstone, which is always more believable when it's screamed in your face, or so he thought. He used to say those numbers now and again, like he was taunting someone. A very odd duck, the A-postle. I'm glad he's gone."

I made her back up and tell me more. Had he said anything else about the numbers?

"This can't lead to anything good."

"It led to forty million in gold last time."

Not a bad answer, if I do say so myself.

Gladys let out a deep breath and shook her head.

"He didn't just say the numbers, he said something more. He'd be preaching along like he always did with that Bible in his hand and suddenly he'd stop and yell 'three-one-one door goes SLAM and you're dead!' And he'd slam his hand on the Bible real hard. No one liked him."

"So I've heard."

Gladys shot me an accusing look and I knew I'd gotten dangerously close to her Crossbones radar. Before she could start asking me questions, I hightailed it for the shop.

When I got back, I found two out-of-towners standing outside looking for free fishing tips. I steered them in the right direction as fast as I could, then jumped on the shop computer and typed the Apostle's phrase into Google.

311 door goes SLAM and you're dead!

It felt all wrong typing it in there, like I'd said some sort of incantation and the ghost of

OLD JOE BUSH WAS ABOUT TO WANDER IN, SUMMONED FROM THE DEAD.

But Google felt differently about those words. It returned a link that made me whisper the word <u>BINGO</u> the second I saw it.

<u>Haunted High Schools</u>

About ten seconds later, I gave up on the idea of not using the shop phone to call Sarah.

311 WAS A CLASSROOM NUMBER AT A HIGH SCHOOL
BUILT IN THE 1800s. THE ROOM WAS SAID TO BE
HAUNTED. THE DOOR LOCKED ON ITS OWN.
UNEXPLAINED SOUNDS CAME FROM INSIDE WHEN NO ONE
ELSE COULD GET IN. THIS WAS ALL VERY INTERESTING,
AND, EVEN BETTER, NOW I KNEW WHERE THE APOSTLE
HAD HIDDEN WHAT WE NEEDED TO FIND. AND IT WASN'T
INSIDE THE SCHOOL, IT WAS OUTSIDE, WHERE SARAH
COULD GET TO IT WITHOUT BEING SEEN (I HOPED).

Remove the Key
in Lamp marked 3.
Go to 4 and open
the door...
2.

REMOVE THE KEY IN LAMP MARKED 3. GO TO
4 AND OPEN THE DOOR. . . .

I KNEW WHAT THIS MEANT, AND IT WAS GOOD!
THERE MUST BE LIGHTS OUTSIDE, ONES THAT HAD
BEEN THERE A LONG TIME. SARAH WOULDN'T HAVE TO
WAIT UNTIL MORNING; IN FACT, THAT WOULD BE EXACTLY

WHAT SHE <u>WOULDN'T</u> WANT TO DO. SHE'D NEED TO SNEAK ONTO THE GROUNDS WHEN IT WAS DARK, FIND THE LAMP MARKED <u>3</u> (WHATEVER THAT MEANT), GET THE KEY, AND PROCEED TO THE NUMBER <u>4</u>, WHERE SHE'D OPEN THE DOOR. THIS CLUE WOULD BE A LOT BETTER IF IT MADE SENSE, BUT SARAH IS SHARP ON HER FEET AFTER MIDNIGHT, SO THERE'S A CHANCE SHE'LL FIGURE IT OUT. AND THIS TIME, I'LL BE RIGHT THERE WITH HER.

THE ONE REALLY BAD THING ABOUT ROOM 311? IT'S IN SPRINGFIELD, MISSOURI, WHICH IS IN THE OPPOSITE DIRECTION OF THE WAY SARAH HAS BEEN DRIVING ALL DAY.

SHE PICKED UP HER PHONE AND STARTED IN ON ME BEFORE I COULD TELL HER WHAT I'D FOUND.

"WHERE HAVE YOU BEEN? DO YOU HAVE ANY IDEA HOW MANY TIMES I'VE TRIED TO CALL? NOT A GOOD TIME TO LEAVE ME HANGING, RYAN. NOT A GOOD TIME!"

I APOLOGIZED ABOUT FIFTY TIMES AND TOLD HER WHAT HAD HAPPENED WITH MY DAD. MY DAD WAS ONTO US, OR AT LEAST GETTING SUSPICIOUS, AND WE NEEDED TO BE CAREFUL. ONCE I GOT HER SETTLED DOWN, SHE WAS JUST HAPPY TO HEAR MY VOICE, WHICH MADE <u>ME</u>

HAPPY. IT WAS LIKE WE WERE THE ONLY TWO PEOPLE IN THE WORLD, SECRETLY GOING ABOUT OUR BUSINESS. IT WAS A GOOD FEELING, BUT IT ALSO MADE ME MISS HER MORE THAN EVER.

WHAT I REALLY WANTED TO DO? JUMP IN MY MOM'S MINIVAN AND DRIVE IN SARAH'S DIRECTION UNTIL WE COLLIDED. I'D HAVE DRIVEN THIRTY HOURS STRAIGHT TO FIND HER IF I THOUGHT I COULD GET AWAY WITH IT.

I HEARD NOISE IN THE BACKGROUND AND ASKED SARAH WHERE SHE WAS, BRACING MYSELF FOR THE BAD NEWS.

HOW FAR COULD SHE HAVE GOTTEN? HOW MUCH TIME HAD WE LOST?

"STEAK 'N SHAKE," SHE SAID. "THE FUNNY THING ABOUT THIS PLACE? I DON'T THINK THEY MAKE STEAKS. PRETTY GOOD GRILLED CHEESE, THOUGH."

ALL THESE WEIRD RESTAURANTS! WHERE ARE THE MCDONALD'S AND THE BURGER KINGS?

"TONIGHT I'M HITTING THE CRACKER BARREL FOR ALL-NIGHT BREAKFAST. THAT PLACE MAKES A MEAN OMELET."

"WHAT STEAK 'N SHAKE ARE YOU AT? I MEAN, WHAT CITY?"

"MEMPHIS. I'M AHEAD OF SCHEDULE BY HALF AN HOUR."

I HEARD HER SLURPING ON A MILK SHAKE AND WANTED TO GUESS WHAT FLAVOR IT WAS, BUT TIME WAS OF THE ESSENCE. (I'D HAVE GUESSED CHOCOLATE.)

"LOOK, SARAH, I'VE GOT SOME GOOD NEWS AND SOME BAD NEWS," I TOLD HER. I WENT ON TO GIVE HER THE SAME GOOD AND BAD NEWS I'VE ALREADY WRITTEN DOWN ONCE BEFORE, AND SHE SORT OF FREAKED OUT ON ME.

"CENTRAL HIGH SCHOOL IN <u>WHERE</u>?"

"SPRINGFIELD, MISSOURI."

"HANG ON."

I HEARD HER SET THE PHONE DOWN ON THE COUNTER AND RIFFLE THROUGH SOME PAPERS, PROBABLY MAPS OF THE REGION. A FEW SECONDS LATER, SHE WAS BACK.

"THAT'S THREE HUNDRED MILES IN THE OPPOSITE DIRECTION, BUT AT LEAST IT'S NOT IN MONTANA. THINGS COULD BE A LOT WORSE."

SOME WEIRD PART OF ME WANTED TO REMIND HER THAT THE BEST FLY-FISHING IN THE WORLD WAS IN MONTANA, AND I'D HAVE BEEN HAPPY TO BOLT OUT THERE AND CATCH A FEW FISH WHILE ACTUALLY MAKING myself useful to our little endeavor, but I let it slide. We figured out it would take five hours for her to drive from Memphis to Springfield, by which time it would be late at night. She was supposed to be in Little Rock before dark, but that wasn't going to happen.

"I'll cover," she said. "I don't think my parents will send the cavalry just yet."

We made a plan: Sarah would leave straight away for Springfield and find the hotel nearest to the school. While she drove, I'd figure out what she should do when she got inside. Tomorrow morning she'd get into the school as early as possible, then head for Little Rock a day late.

"Sorry, Sarah, this isn't going quite like I thought it would."

"Funny, it's going EXACTLY how I expected. That's what makes it perfect! Don't worry — this is going to be great. You're doing recon, I'm out in the field — we make a perfect team."

I understand what she meant, but deep down inside, I still feel like such a loser. I wish I could

BE THE ONE TO DRIVE ALL NIGHT, CHASING DOWN URBAN LEGENDS, FUELED ON HAMBURGERS AND MILK SHAKES. BEING BORED IS ONE THING, BUT FEELING TRAPPED IS A WHOLE DIFFERENT LEVEL OF LAMENESS. SARAH IS OUT THERE, LIVING LARGE, AND WHAT AM I DOING? TYING A BUNCH OF STUPID FLIES AND WATCHING THE PAINT DRY.

WE TALKED ABOUT THE PHRASE WITH THE LAMP AND THE NUMBERS AND SHE AGREED: SHE'D HAVE TO GET OVER THERE AT NIGHT, WHEN NO ONE WAS AROUND.

"TONIGHT, HAUNTED SCHOOL, SPRINGFIELD," SARAH SAID. I COULD TELL SHE WAS UP AND MOVING. "I CAN HARDLY WAIT."

AND THEN SHE WAS GONE. I STILL HAVE FIFTY-NINE FLIES TO TIE. SARAH HAS HER PARENTS TO FOOL AND A FIVE-HOUR DRIVE TO NAVIGATE. WITH ANY LUCK AT ALL, WE'LL BOTH SUCCEED BY THE TIME MY DAD GETS OFF THE RIVER AND GIVES ME MY PHONE BACK.

WEDNESDAY, JUNE 22, 8:45 P.M.

I just got a call from Fitz that under normal circumstances would put me in a pretty good mood. The call could only mean one thing, which was perfectly clear by the frustrated sound of Fitz's voice.

"The hatch totally died. Slowest day on the river in weeks. Talk about some unhappy fishermen."

"That bad?" I asked him.

"You have no idea. We could have thrown worms slathered in WD-40 out there and it would have produced the same result: NADA."

Legend in our neck of the woods is that fish love WD-40 more than life itself. They'd beat each other up trying to hook themselves, but I'd never tried it.

This was tailor-made for gloating rights. I go out and catch fish after fish, Fitz heads out the very next day and gets skunked. It should have been music to my ears, but my pile of flies was only sixty-one deep. I had thirty-five to go and my fingers were already raw from tying.

"BETTER LUCK NEXT TIME," WAS ALL I COULD MUSTER.

"WE'LL BE BACK AT THE SHOP IN ABOUT TWENTY. WANT SOME HELP FINISHING THOSE FLIES?"

FITZ DIDN'T HAVE TO ASK IF I'D FINISHED — HE'D SEEN MY WORK BEFORE AND KNEW THE RESULTS ALL TOO WELL. HE GUESSED I'D FINISHED SEVENTY, WHICH MADE ME FEEL EVEN WORSE THAN I ALREADY DID. AT LEAST MY NIGHT WAS GOING TO END A LITTLE EARLIER THAN EXPECTED AND I COULD GET MY PHONE BACK.

IT'S COOL FITZ IS WILLING TO HELP ME OUT, ESPECIALLY AFTER I SHOWED HIM UP ON THE RIVER.

HERE'S HOPING I CAN HIT SEVENTY BEFORE HE WALKS IN THE DOOR.

When he got back, I traded Fitz jobs, unloading and cleaning the boats while he whipped off twenty-six flies in record time. My dad was none the wiser. I guess if Fitz and I were truly competitive, he would've found a way to let my dad know. But everything remained between us. When Fitz was through, he told me to keep practicing on those flies, and I told him to keep practicing on that fishing. Then he got on his old motorcycle and took off, a stream of blue smoke trailing him in the moonlight. I knew just how he felt — I'd been there. Nothing makes you more tired than rowing a boat all day and listening to people complain about not catching fish. It's murder.

Before I could get my phone back from my dad, he looked at my fly-tying handiwork and found some of it wanting. I had to admit — there were twenty-six perfect little guys in the pile, but the rest were gimps. Half of them probably wouldn't even float.

"I could spray them with WD-40," I said lamely, hoping to get him smiling.

He handed me my phone and smiled.

"Can't be good at everything. I think Fitz is bad luck on the water. Worst day of the year."

I feel bad about how good it felt to hear my dad say that. It isn't fair to Fitz, but I sure don't want to get in the habit of sitting around the shop all summer when I could be out fishing. Fitz could tie, and it was starting to look like I'm "good luck" on the river.

Now if only that good luck could make its way to Springfield, Missouri.

I have no doubt that Sarah needs it.

By the time I finally called Sarah she was sitting in her car across the street from the school. She'd been waiting a while and was impatient, so our conversation was brief. A minute after I reached her, Sarah was wandering on the grounds searching the bottom of every lamppost she could find. Some of them were new, because the school had been added on to, but there was an entire wing that still had the old facade and a few statues of patriarchs that Sarah said "looked real, like they were planning to climb off their pedestals and drag me down the street."

She found a row of lampposts that looked like they could have been placed there quite a while ago, and then she was feeding me information that felt right.

"Okay, there's a bunch of these, like eight or so, and they have big bases on them. It's like they're tall and skinny, but wide at the bottom. They're not numbered, but they're in a row. That's good, right?"

I TOLD HER TO COUNT FROM ONE END OF THE ROW UNTIL SHE GOT TO THE THIRD ONE, THEN SEE IF THERE WAS SOME SORT OF LATCH OR METAL DOOR AT THE BASE.

"DANG IT," SHE SAID, LOUDER THAN I THOUGHT WAS A GOOD IDEA.

THERE WAS A SMALL METAL DOOR, PROBABLY FOR GETTING ACCESS TO THE WIRING, BUT IT REQUIRED ONE OF THOSE ALLEN WRENCHES TO GET IN. SARAH CURSED HERSELF FOR NOT BRINGING TOOLS, THEN RAN ACROSS THE SCHOOL GROUNDS TO HER CAR, WHERE SHE KEPT A TOOLBOX IN THE TRUNK.

AFTER WHAT SEEMED LIKE AN HOUR, SHE RETURNED TO THE LAMPPOST, FUMBLED AROUND WITH A BUNCH OF DIFFERENT SIZES, AND FOUND THE RIGHT ONE. WHEN SHE FINALLY GOT IT OPEN, SHE PUT HER HAND INSIDE AND FELT AROUND.

"IT FEELS LIKE I MIGHT GET ELECTROCUTED IN THERE," SHE TOLD ME. "CAN YOU SAY FRANKENSTEIN?"

I HAD A TERRIBLE URGE TO TELL HER THE ELECTROCUTION BIT IS ONLY IN THE MOVIE, NOT IN THE BOOK, BUT THIS WAS PROBABLY NOT THE RIGHT TIME TO GO ALL LITERARY ON MY BEST FRIEND. I CONTROLLED

MY URGE TO TALK ABOUT MARY SHELLEY AND STUCK
TO THE BUSINESS AT HAND, WHICH WAS GETTING SARAH
OUT OF HARM'S WAY AS FAST AS I COULD.

"JUST BE CAREFUL — IT'S NOT GOING TO HURT YOU."

"EASY FOR YOU TO SAY. YOU'RE AT HOME WITH
THE DOORS LOCKED AND I'M SEARCHING THE GROUNDS
OF A HAUNTED SCHOOL."

"POINT TAKEN. TRY REACHING UP INTO THE SPACE
WHERE NO ONE WOULD EVER THINK TO FIND SOMETHING."

I COULD HEAR HER DOING HER BEST, IMAGINED HER
ARM IN THERE UP TO HER ELBOW AS SHE TRIED TO FIND
A HIDDEN KEY. WHAT IF SHE REALLY DID GET
ELECTROCUTED? WHAT IF THERE WERE LOOSE WIRES
IN THERE AND SHE FRIED HER WHOLE DANG ARM OFF?

"GOT IT!" SHE YELLED. WHEW.

I YELLED "NICE!" A LITTLE TOO LOUD AND MY
MOM WOKE UP. I COULD TELL, BECAUSE SHE SHOUTED
"YOU OKAY, RYAN?" DOWN THE HALL.

I DIDN'T ANSWER. MY MOM IS A HEAVY SLEEPER,
AND SHE HATES TO GET OUT OF BED AT NIGHT. ONCE
SHE'S UP, SHE'S UP FOR LIKE AN HOUR. I COULD IMAGINE
HER STARING AT THE CEILING, HOPING SHE'D ONLY
THOUGHT SHE'D HEARD ME YELL, HOPING SHE COULD

STAY WHERE SHE WAS. SARAH WAS YAMMERING IN MY EAR BUT I STAYED PERFECTLY STILL AND QUIET. WHAT IF MY MOM WAS SNEAKING DOWN THE HALL, STANDING AT MY DOOR? I WATCHED FOR A SHADOW UNDER THE DOOR FOR A FULL MINUTE, THEN BREATHED A SIGH OF RELIEF. SHE HAD TO BE ASLEEP AGAIN.

SARAH HAD FOUND A SMALL METAL BOX, HELD INSIDE ON A HOOK, UP WHERE NO ONE WOULD EVER HAVE A REASON TO LOOK.

THIS WAS GETTING GOOD.

I WHISPERED TO HER, "MOM'S ON ALERT, GOTTA STAY LOW. LISTEN, THOSE STATUES OF PEOPLE, HOW MANY ARE THERE?"

"I WAS THINKING THE SAME THING, AND YOU'RE RIGHT — THERE ARE FOUR."

"THEN YOU KNOW WHAT TO DO."

REMOVE THE KEY IN LAMP MARKED 3. GO TO 4 AND OPEN THE DOOR. . . .

I HEARD SARAH RUNNING, HER BREATH HEAVIER THAN IT NEEDED TO BE. SHE WAS STARTING TO GET SCARED OR NERVOUS, I COULD TELL. I TALKED HER DOWN, TRIED TO MAKE HER FEEL BETTER, BUT SHE WAS STARTING TO FEEL THE PRESSURE.

"I don't like it out here, Ryan. Something doesn't feel right."

"Just stay calm. You can do it. There must be some sort of small door with a key entry somewhere at the base."

She told me there was, but that her hands were shaking so badly she couldn't get the key in. Also, the keyhole was totally blocked with crusted old chewing gum.

"Use the smallest Allen wrench you've got and clean it out."

This was a good tip, because a ring of Allen wrenches has sizes that are like metal toothpicks, perfect for clearing away old gum.

"Someone's here. I can feel it. I'm turning my camera on."

I tried to tell her no, just stay focused on the keyhole, but she wouldn't listen.

Everything went quiet. I called her name, but there was nothing. Even her breathing had stopped.

Then the phone went dead.

I TRIED CALLING BACK TWICE, BUT IT WENT STRAIGHT TO VOICE MAIL. I PACED IN MY ROOM. WAS SHE SEEING THINGS? WAS THERE REALLY SOMEONE OUT THERE? WHAT WAS GOING ON?

MY PHONE BUZZED WITH A TEXT MESSAGE.

HE'S HERE.

I TYPED BACK AS FAST AS MY FINGERS WOULD FLY.

WHO? GET OUT OF THERE!

HER REPLY WAS THE LAST THING I WANTED TO SEE. EVER.

OLD JOE BUSH. HE'S HERE.

THIS WAS AS CLOSE AS I'VE EVER COME TO SCREAMING IN MY ROOM. ACTUALLY, I DID SCREAM, BUT I GOT MY PILLOW FIRST AND HELD IT AGAINST MY FACE.

A FEW SECONDS LATER, MY PHONE RANG, AND SARAH WAS BACK.

"TELL ME YOU WERE MESSING WITH ME. PLEASE, SARAH, TELL ME YOU WERE KIDDING."

"I'M BACK IN MY CAR. I'M SAFE, BUT I WASN'T KIDDING. HE WAS THERE, RYAN. HE WAS RIGHT THERE, STANDING IN THE SHADOWS."

"It could have been anyone." I said these words more out of hope than reality. I knew Old Joe Bush was still out there. I'd seen him myself.

"My camera was on, so I'll show you. Right now, I'm getting out of here. This is crazy, Ryan. Like really crazy."

And then she started laughing. She was thrilled and scared to death all at once. Sarah Fincher loved this kind of ride, where the stakes were high and the shocks were off the charts. But even this one got to her more than usual. She was laughing, but it was a hair shy of turning into crying. I knew her well enough to know that much.

Someone was watching us. Someone knew.

And that someone was out there with my friend, keeping an eye on what was his.

"I got it. I got what we were supposed to find."

Those were the last words Sarah said before stepping into the hotel lobby.

SARAH WAS CALM WHEN SHE CALLED BACK FIFTEEN MINUTES LATER. SHE WAS IN HER HOTEL ROOM, AND I COULD TELL SHE'D HIT THE WALL. SHE WAS SAFELY TUCKED AWAY IN A LOCKED ROOM. WE BOTH FELT BETTER.

SHE'D GOTTEN THE SMALL METAL DOOR OPEN AND HAD FOUND ANOTHER SMALL REEL OF FILM, WHICH MEANT THE APOSTLE WAS ABOUT TO START TALKING AGAIN.

AND THERE WAS SOMETHING ELSE.

SARAH'S PARENTS WERE MORE UPSET THAN SHE'D EXPECTED, AND THEY WANTED TO KNOW EXACTLY WHERE SHE WAS AND WHY SHE'D DRIFTED OFF COURSE.

"NOT A GREAT PHONE CALL EARLIER TONIGHT," SHE TOLD ME. "I THOUGHT THEY WERE GOING TO MAKE ME TURN AROUND AND HEAD BACK HOME."

SHE'D CALLED THEM AT AROUND 9:00 TO TELL THEM SHE'D MADE A MISTAKE IN ST. LOUIS AND WAS HEADED TOWARD SPRINGFIELD INSTEAD OF LITTLE ROCK, BUT HADN'T REALIZED IT UNTIL SHE FOUND HERSELF FOUR HOURS OFF COURSE.

"The part that stung the most was them thinking I was actually that dumb," she went on. "I mean, seriously, do they really think I'd drive four hours in the wrong direction without doing it on purpose?"

They weren't "onto us," as I'd been so worried about. No, they were something far worse in Sarah's book: They were worried their daughter was an idiot. I tried to convince her that having her parents think she's dumb is actually kind of useful in this particular situation.

"You can make as many mistakes as you want. They'll just think you have a bad sense of direction."

"Ryan, you don't get it," she corrected me. "This was the only slipup they're going to allow. They got me a hotel room here, but only after grilling the front desk lady like she was a convicted felon. So embarrassing. If this happens again they're pulling the plug. My dad said so."

Not good. Not good at all, since there were

AT LEAST A COUPLE MORE TIMES ON THIS JOURNEY WHERE SHOWING UP ON TIME WOULD REQUIRE A SMALL MIRACLE.

She was road weary. Too much junk food, too many headlights in the face, and not nearly enough sleep had pushed Sarah to the brink.

Now I'm exhausted, too. It's time to get some sleep.

If I can.

Thursday, June 23, 8:00 a.m.

Sarah was up very early. I can tell because she posted another video before hitting the road for Little Rock.

This thing is scary in so many ways.

There's her troubling documentary about the words 311 door goes SLAM and you're dead! I never liked that phrase to begin with, but now I don't want to hear it again for as long as I live.

Then there's a new message from the A-postle, which is stranger than the first.

But the most terrible part, by a mile, was what her camera caught while she was at the school. I had no idea what she'd seen. She hadn't told me. Nope, not good old Sarah — she had wanted to show me so I could be just as scared as she was.

This video changed everything, and I don't recommend continuing with this journal until you see it.

The stakes just got a lot higher.

SARAHFINCHER.COM
PASSWORD:
SLAM

THURSDAY, JUNE 23, 9:24 A.M.

I UNDERSTAND WHY SHE DIDN'T TELL ME. I THINK SHE WAS IN SHOCK, BUT ALSO I THINK SHE THOUGHT SERIOUSLY ABOUT TURNING FOR HOME. SHE SAYS SHE'S ON HER WAY TO LITTLE ROCK, THAT SHE'LL TAKE A BREAK WHEN SHE GETS THERE AND DECIDE IF SHE WANTS TO KEEP GOING. SHE'LL BE THERE BY EARLY AFTERNOON, GET SOME REAL REST — AND THEN WHAT? TURN FOR BOSTON OR AUSTIN, TEXAS? HOME IS SAFE. AUSTIN IS THE DRISKILL, THE MOST HAUNTED HOTEL IN AMERICA. I'D ENCOURAGE HER TO QUIT AND GO HOME OR JUST DRIVE STRAIGHT THROUGH TO UCLA AND FORGET ABOUT THE APOSTLE AND EVERYTHING ELSE.

BUT I KNOW SHE WON'T LISTEN TO ME.

NEITHER ONE OF US CAN TURN BACK NOW.

WE'RE IN TOO DEEP.

I'M NOT GOING TO TAKE THE TIME TO RECAP THE DOCUMENTARY FOOTAGE ABOUT THE SCHOOL — THAT'S GOING TO STAY IN VIDEO FORM ONLY. BUT I WILL LAY OUT THE NEW INFORMATION WE HAVE ABOUT THE CROSSBONES AND THE MESSAGE THE GHOST OF OLD JOE BUSH SENT.

First Joe, then the Crossbones.

I've heard of these things that are like benevolent spirits, ghosts who are there to protect or warn us, not to bring us harm. If I believe in ghosts at all, I sure want to believe in that kind. Here's what it said: <u>I'm not here to harm you. Quite the opposite. Keep going, but tell no one. It would only anger him more. You've awakened the Raven.</u>

Okay, first off, who the heck is the Raven? I know the poem, and Sarah has used it as a password, but apparently the Raven is also a person or a being of sorts who's angry at us. Just what we need — a giant black bird gunning for us. What if it's bigger than me? I don't even want to think about the beak on a Raven that big.

The most interesting thing about that footage, though? Old Joe Bush might be on our side. I've had some experience with this sort of thing, and it adds up. Henry pretended to be the ghost of Old Joe Bush, but that doesn't mean the ghost never existed to begin with. Whether this thing has taken over Henry or Henry isn't

EVEN IN THE PICTURE AND THIS GHOST IS REAL, THE SAME THING IS TRUE: THE REAL JOE BUSH WAS A GOOD GUY. HE WAS ALL ABOUT PROTECTING THE TOWN FROM THE VERY BEGINNING.

I THINK HE'S TRYING TO PROTECT ME AND SARAH NOW.

BUT PROTECT US FROM WHAT?

THE RAVEN — WHATEVER OR WHOEVER THAT IS.

SECTION TWO OF THE FOUR SECTIONS OF THE PUZZLE SHOWED ITSELF IN THE VIDEO, JUST AS THE FIRST ONE HAD. THE WORD IS <u>GROUND</u>. PUT IT TOGETHER WITH THE FIRST WORD, <u>UNDER</u>, AND IT MAKES ANOTHER WORD: UNDER — GROUND. <u>UNDERGROUND</u>.

IT DOES <u>NOT</u> HAVE A NICE RING TO IT.

THE LAST PLACE I WANT TO BE WHEN THIS THING GOES DOWN IS UNDERGROUND.

AS TO THE CROSSBONES, IT GETS WEIRDER BY TURNS, AND SO DOES THE APOSTLE. IT'S CLEAR TO ME NOW THAT THE APOSTLE WAS NEAR THE TOP OF THE CROSSBONES HIERARCHY AND TOOK IT UPON HIMSELF TO DOCUMENT WHAT HE KNEW. ALSO, HE WAS DISGRUNTLED. THESE CLUES HE'S LEFT ARE SOME SORT OF INSURANCE AGAINST THE CROSSBONES, A WAY OF saying, HEY, TREAT ME WITH SOME RESPECT OR I'LL TELL EVERYONE WHAT YOU'VE DONE. MY FINGER IS ON THE TRIGGER, SO DON'T MESS WITH ME.

THE A-POSTLE VIDEO ALSO CONNECTS THE CROSSBONES TO THOMAS JEFFERSON, WHOM THEY DISTRUSTED. THEY WANTED TO DESTROY THE FORMER PRESIDENT, TRYING ON THREE OCCASIONS: SETTING HIS HOUSE ON FIRE, DRIVING HIM INTO BANKRUPTCY, AND — THE THIRD ITEM IS ONLY HINTED AT, BUT IT SOUNDS LIKE IT HAS SOMETHING TO DO WITH TAKING JEFFERSON'S ASSETS. AND FINALLY, THE A-POSTLE HAS OPENED THE DOOR TO THE DREDGE AND WHY IT MATTERED. THE NEW YORK GOLD AND SILVER COMPANY WAS A CROSSBONES INVENTION. ALL THAT GOLD, INCLUDING THE RICHES DUG OUT OF SKELETON CREEK, WAS CROSSBONES GOLD.

I THINK THE A-POSTLE WANTED MORE THAN THEY WERE WILLING TO GIVE HIM. HE GOT GREEDY.

UNFORTUNATELY FOR HIM, HE MIGHT HAVE BEEN A LITTLE TOO LOUD FOR HIS OWN GOOD.

HE ENDED UP FLOATING FACEDOWN IN THE RIVER, AND WHO TOOK CREDIT FOR THAT LITTLE "ACCIDENT"?

HENRY.

LITTLE DOUBT REMAINS: HENRY AND THE APOSTLE
WERE BIG-TIME MEMBERS OF THE CROSSBONES.
THEY WERE ENEMIES IN THE END.

IF THERE WERE THREE AT THE TOP OF THIS
SHADOWY ORGANIZATION, I'D HAVE TO GUESS THE THIRD
PERSON WAS THE RAVEN.

THE BIG QUESTION THIS RAISES FOR ME RIGHT NOW:
HOW IS MY DAD INVOLVED?

A BAD THOUGHT HAS ENTERED AND I CAN'T STOP
ROLLING IT OVER IN MY HEAD.

WHAT IF MY DAD IS THE RAVEN?

ME AND FITZ WENT DOWN THE STREET FOR A BURGER AND FRIES AT THE CAFÉ AND TALKED ABOUT FISHING, FISHING, AND MORE FISHING. WHY THE HATCH WAS OFF SO SEVERELY WE DIDN'T EVEN GO OUT TODAY. WHAT MAKES A GOOD FLY AND A BAD FLY (THE PERSON MAKING THEM, OBVIOUSLY), BIGGEST FISH EVER, MOST FISH IN A DAY, AN HOUR, AND A MINUTE (THREE IN ONE MINUTE, ALTHOUGH I THINK HE'S LYING). FITZ COULD TALK ABOUT THE ARCANE BUSINESS OF HOOKING A TROUT LIKE MY MOM COULD TALK ABOUT BON JOVI.

I MENTION THIS BECAUSE MY MOM IS A PRODUCT OF THE 1980s AND SHE WILL NOT STOP LISTENING TO MUSIC FROM HER "ERA." JOURNEY IS A PARTICULAR FAVORITE. ALSO ASIA, DEF LEPPARD, REO SPEEDWAGON, AND STYX. BUT BON JOVI IS THE KING OF '80s ROCK AND ROLL IN MY MOM'S VIEW, THE PERFECT ANTIDOTE AFTER A LONG DAY AT WORK. I'VE HEARD THIS ONE SONG, "LIVIN' ON A PRAYER," AT LEAST FIVE MILLION TIMES.

MY MOM HAS TWO FRIENDS FROM COLLEGE WHO LIVE IN SEATTLE AND THE THREE OF THEM ARE GOING TO A BON JOVI CONCERT NEXT TUESDAY NIGHT. IT'S

ALL MY MOM HAS TALKED ABOUT FOR DAYS, AND I MENTIONED THIS FACT TO FITZ, WHICH PRODUCED A GOOD RESULT:

"THAT DUDE IS LIKE A HUNDRED YEARS OLD, RIGHT? HE MUST HAVE SOLD HIS SOUL TO THE DEVIL."

"ALL I KNOW IS SHE'LL BE GONE MONDAY TO WEDNESDAY AND I'M LOOKING FORWARD TO IT. ME AND DAD EAT OUT, WATCH TV, AND FISH UNTIL MIDNIGHT. IT'LL BE SWEET."

"SOUNDS LIKE HEAVEN. SAY YOU'LL INVITE ME."

"IT'LL COST YOU FOUR DOZEN FLIES WITH MY NAME ON 'EM. BUT YOU CAN'T MAKE THEM PERFECT, THEY HAVE TO BE ALMOST PERFECT. OTHERWISE MY DAD WILL KNOW YOU DID IT FOR ME."

"DEAL."

IT WAS NICE TO KNOW I COULD CASH IN ON FORTY-EIGHT FITZ-TIED FLIES WHENEVER I WANTED. IT REPRESENTED HOURS OF WORK, AND IT WAS TIME I WANTED ACCESS TO IN CASE I GOT LEFT IN THE FLY SHOP ALONE ANYTIME SOON. I THOUGHT ABOUT THAT AND CHANGED TACTICS.

"THIS IS AN UP-FRONT PAYMENT DEAL, FITZ," I CONCLUDED. "I'M GOING TO NEED THOSE FLIES BY

TOMORROW MORNING, JUST TO BE SAFE. NEVER KNOW WHEN I MIGHT NEED THEM."

"THE ONLY PROBLEM I SEE IS MAKING THEM IMPERFECT. THAT'S GONNA REALLY TEST MY SKILLS."

I LIKE FITZ. HE'S INTO THE SAME THINGS I AM AND HE'S FUNNY. I HAVE A FEELING THE NEXT FOOTBALL SEASON WAS GOING TO BE A HOOT WITH THIS GUY DURING THE LONG RIDE ON THE BENCH.

IT'S NOT THE SAME AS HAVING SARAH AROUND, BUT IT'S SOMETHING.

Thursday, June 23, 8:00 p.m.

After the lunch break, my dad and I hit the river for a few hours to see if things had improved and found that they had. We weren't guiding anyone, but the fish were slamming dry flies on the surface of the water again, so things were looking up. Chances were pretty good the weekend would produce some serious fishermen heading in from Boise or even Portland.

Fitz tied all the flies he owed me while we were gone, which shouldn't have surprised me, but it did. He showed the results when my dad wasn't looking and I had a hard time finding the imperfections.

"Trust me, Ryan — these aren't perfect. I'd lose all respect for myself if I gave these to your dad."

"Did I mention we caught more fish than you could shake a stick at?"

"You did, and you're a loser."

Me and Fitz had great shop banter. It was really enjoyable. I had forty-eight flies in my backpack, a friendly doofus for a shop mate, and

A SUCCESSFUL DAY OF FISHING UNDER MY BELT. I COULD ONLY HOPE THAT SARAH HAD ENJOYED HER DAY IN LITTLE ROCK AS MUCH AS I'D ENJOYED MINE IN SKELETON CREEK.

FOR DINNER I WENT HOME AND TALKED TO MY MOM, WHO WAS BLARING BON JOVI ALL THE WAY OUT INTO THE STREET. NO AMOUNT OF BARBECUE IS WORTH THIS TORTURE, AND I TOLD HER AS MUCH WHILE SHE FLIPPED BURGERS.

"NO ONE ELSE IN TOWN WANTS JOE BONJY BLARING DOWN THE STREET THROUGH THE SCREEN DOOR."

I HAD LONG SINCE STOPPED CALLING THIS GUY BY HIS REAL NAME AND MY MOM HATED IT.

"BON JOVI IS A LEGEND. ONE DAY YOU'LL REALIZE THAT AND THANK ME FOR INTRODUCING YOU TO SOME REAL MUSIC."

FAT CHANCE, MOM. CAN I PLEASE JUST GET MY CHEESEBURGER? AND FOR THE SAKE OF TEENAGERS EVERYWHERE, PLEASE STOP DANCING ON THE PORCH.

I WATCHED IN HORROR AS MY MOM RAISED THE SPATULA LIKE A DRUMSTICK AND STARTED WAILING ON THE GRILL, THEN I RETURNED TO DRAWING IN MY JOURNAL. I'D ONLY ENCOURAGED HER BAD BEHAVIOR.

Best to stay quiet until my dad came home and made her shut down the concert.

I had been drawing a map of where Sarah had been, where she was going, and what she was finding. She was making some serious progress, no doubt, but the longest road was ahead of her and it worried me. A day of chilling in Little Rock, Arkansas, might have killed the whole excursion, and she'd been ominously quiet all day. I was giving her some space, not bugging her, letting her off the grid for a few hours.

This is the map I drew:

SARAH'S ROAD TRIP
—7 DAYS!—

DAY 1 - 983 miles / 15 hours
DAY 2 - 820 miles / 14 hours
DAY 3 - 300 miles / 5 hours
DAY 4 - 620 miles / 10 hours
DAY 5 - 950 miles / 15 hours
DAY 6 - 700 miles / 11 hours
DAY 7 - 340 miles / 5 hours

I sat on the porch eating my burger, waving flies off my Doritos.

All I could think of was Sarah.

Will she move toward me or away from me come morning?

MAYBE I SHOULDN'T BE SO EXCITED, BUT I AM — SARAH IS ON THE ROAD AGAIN, AND SHE'S HEADED STRAIGHT FOR AUSTIN, TEXAS. SHE GOT AN EARLY START AND SHOULD ARRIVE AT THE DRISKILL HOTEL BY 5:00 IN THE EVENING. AFTER THAT SHE'LL NEED TO KEEP GOING UNTIL SHE REACHES SAN ANTONIO, WHERE ANOTHER ONE OF MRS. FINCHER'S SIBLINGS LIVES. MRS. FINCHER COMES FROM A BIG FAMILY: THREE SISTERS, TWO BROTHERS. THEY SCATTERED LIKE BUCKSHOT OUT OF SKELETON CREEK YEARS AGO, WHICH, SO FAR, HAS BEEN REALLY CONVENIENT FOR SARAH.

THIS IS REALLY WORKING — WE'RE DOING IT. OR MORE ACCURATELY, SARAH IS DOING IT. I'M LIKE A FAR-REMOVED COPILOT AND IT'S KILLING ME MORE EVERY DAY. WHAT I WANT MORE THAN ANYTHING IN THE WORLD IS TO BE OUT THERE WITH HER, OR EVEN OUT THERE GOING IN A DIFFERENT DIRECTION — ANYTHING THAT WILL GET ME OUT OF THIS TOWN AND INTO SOMETHING EXCITING.

I'M STARTING TO SOUND MORE LIKE SARAH EVERY DAY, AND THAT'S FINE BY ME. THE PEOPLE, THE MUSIC,

THE LONG, BORING DAYS IN THE FLY SHOP — I GUESS IT'S ALL STARTING TO DRIVE ME MAD WITH ROAD TRIP ENVY.

We've DONE OUR RESEARCH ON THE DRISKILL, AND SARAH WARNED ME THAT GETTING A DOCUMENTARY ABOUT IT WAS KIND OF UNLIKELY SINCE SHE'S GOING TO BE GETTING INTO SAN ANTONIO LATE AND RIGHT BACK ON THE ROAD SATURDAY MORNING FOR THE LONG HAUL TO PHOENIX. AFTER THAT, IT WAS ANOTHER LONG DRIVE TO SAN JOSE FOR THE FINAL LOCATION — THE WINCHESTER HOUSE — AND THEN SHE'D HAVE TO MAKE IT BACK TO LA FOR THE START OF FILM SCHOOL ON MONDAY AT 10:00 A.M. AN ALL-NIGHTER WOULD BE REQUIRED SOMEWHERE IN THERE OR SHE'D NEVER MAKE IT.

My DAD SURPRISED ME WITH WHAT I'M SURE HE THOUGHT WAS STUNNINGLY GOOD NEWS, BUT IT WAS MORE OF A MIXED BAG THAN HE REALIZED.

"SOMEONE WENT BACK TO BOISE AND SPILLED THE BEANS ABOUT THAT DAY WE HAD LAST WEEK. YOU KNOW, LUNKER DAY," MY DAD BEGAN. HE WAS EATING STEEL-CUT OATS, A NEW HABIT TO OFFSET THE GREASY SUMMER BARBECUE FARE WE'D BEEN ENJOYING. "GROUP of four emailed this morning. They bit on the multiday."

"When?" I asked.

"Tuesday and Wednesday — the fish better be biting."

My dad had put together this insane two-day fishing package with streamside camping along a seventeen-mile stretch of river. Under normal circumstances I'd sooner die then have him pick Fitz to man the second boat and serve the fried chicken, but this time, I couldn't think of anything I wanted less.

"Your mom will be in Seattle at that concert, so I can hardly leave you home. You got the gig. We'll leave Fitz in the shop and he'll tie a million flies while we're gone."

My heart sank. Not only was I going to have to take back my invitation to Fitz and give back all the imperfect flies he'd tied for me, I was going to be on the river at a critical time. What if Sarah needed me and I was totally out of range for two days? She was scheduled to be at film camp by then — but still, knowing Sarah,

If there was a fifth location, she'd call in sick for a day or two and off she'd go.

I knew my dad better than to question his decision. If I offered up Fitz, he'd dig in his heels and use his stern voice: <u>Oh, you're going. Don't even try to get out of it.</u>

Then he dropped another bombshell.

"Talked to Sarah's dad last night. How come you didn't mention Sarah was driving across America all by herself?"

I had to think on my feet, because for some unknown, stupid reason I had never prepared for this particular moment.

"That's just the kind of thing she does, Dad. I talk to her when she gets bored, but it's her deal. Speaking of which — I do have a license, you know. How come I never get to drive across the country?"

Put some humor in there, that's the ticket.

My mom actually laughed out loud at that one, like I'd lost my mind. My dad reeled off all the reasons why I wasn't driving anywhere far away soon, and how I should appreciate the

DRIVING I DID GET TO DO: <u>SHE'S A YEAR OLDER THAN</u> <u>YOU, HER PARENTS ARE IDIOTS, SHE'S GOT FAMILY</u> <u>STREWN ALL OVER THE DANG COUNTRY, BE HAPPY YOU</u> <u>GET TO DRIVE THE TRUCK TO THE RIVER.</u>

THIS WAS GOOD. I HAD EFFECTIVELY DIVERTED THEIR ATTENTION AWAY FROM MY OVERAMBITIOUS DRIVING FRIEND AND ONTO THEIR CONCERNS ABOUT ME DRIVING AT ALL. MISSION ACCOMPLISHED, FOR THE MOMENT. MY DAD GAVE ME THAT SUSPICIOUS LOOK AGAIN, BUT HE ALSO HAD <u>TROUT BUM</u> WRITTEN ALL OVER HIS FACE. THERE WAS A LOT TO PLAN WITH AN OVERNIGHTER, AND HIS WHEELS WERE TURNING. NOT ENOUGH ROOM IN THAT HEAD OF HIS FOR TOO MANY BIG THINGS, AND FOR THE MOMENT, HIS BURGEONING BUSINESS WAS TAKING PRECEDENCE OVER WORRYING ABOUT SOME CRAZY TEENAGER DRIVING IN OUR GENERAL DIRECTION.

FRIDAY, JUNE 24, 2:00 P.M.

MY DAD FELT SORRY FOR FITZ AND TOOK HIM OUT ON THE RIVER ALL DAY, BUT NOT BEFORE SPILLING THE BEANS ABOUT NEXT WEEK'S TRIP. FITZ THREATENED TO TAKE HIS FLIES BACK, BUT WHEN I HANDED THEM OVER AND HE TOOK A LONG LOOK AT THEM, HIS FACE SOURED. HE'S A REAL FLY SNOB.

"KEEP 'EM. YOU'RE GOING TO NEED A LOT OF GEAR ON THAT OVERNIGHTER."

MY DAD HAD ALREADY ASSIGNED ANOTHER FOUR DOZEN FOR THE DAY, SO THIS WAS MUSIC TO MY EARS. WITH FITZ'S IMPERFECTS IN HAND, I COULD LOUNGE AROUND ALL DAY IF I WANTED TO, HELP THE OCCASIONAL CUSTOMER, AND BASICALLY CHILL UNTIL SARAH SHOWED UP IN AUSTIN AT AROUND 3:00 P.M. MY TIME.

THEY PULLED OUT OF THE SHOP PARKING LOT AT NOON, AND I STARTED DOING SOME SERIOUS RESEARCH ON THE DRISKILL HOTEL. SINCE SARAH WON'T BE DOING A DOCUMENTARY ON THIS, I'M RECORDING MY FINDINGS HERE, WHILE IT'S STILL LIGHT AND I'M FEELING REASONABLY SAFE.

I'VE PREVIOUSLY MENTIONED THE PART ABOUT THE MIRRORS AND HOW LOOKING INTO THEM WILL REFLECT

THIS DEAD LADY WHO WILL LATER APPEAR IN YOUR NIGHTMARES FOR THE REST OF YOUR LIFE. SORRY, I WANTED TO SCREAM THAT, BECAUSE IT'S JUST SO WRONG. ANYWAY, THE DEAD LADY IN YOUR DREAMS IS ONLY THE HALF OF IT. THE DRISKILL HAS HAD MORE CONFIRMED PARANORMAL EVENTS THAN JUST ABOUT ANY OTHER PLACE IN THE COUNTRY. HERE ARE A FEW OF THE CREEPIER ONES:

— THERE WAS A KID WHO STAYED THERE A LONG TIME AGO WHO HAD THIS RED BOUNCY BALL. SHE SNUCK OUT OF HER PARENTS' ROOM AND STARTED BOUNCING IT DOWN THIS TREMENDOUSLY LONG STAIRCASE, THEN SHE FELL ALL THE WAY TO THE BOTTOM AND BROKE HER NECK. I GUESS SHE WAS ALL TANGLED UP AT THE BOTTOM, VERY GRUESOME. NOW THE SECOND-FLOOR LADIES' ROOM, THE STAIRCASE, AND THE LOBBY ARE HAUNTED BY THE SOUND OF A BOUNCING BALL AND A GIRL WHISPERING IN YOUR EAR.
— THE ORIGINAL OWNER OF THE HOTEL LOVED THE PLACE BUT WENT TOTALLY BANKRUPT

TRYING TO BUILD IT. THE GUY SMOKED CIGARS LIKE A MADMAN, AND SOMETIMES THE SMELL OF SMOKE JUST SHOWS UP IN DIFFERENT PARTS OF THE HOTEL FOR NO REASON WHATSOEVER. CIGAR SMOKE. IT'S A NONSMOKING HOTEL.

— THE HOUSTON BRIDE IS ANOTHER CONFIRMED SIGHTING. SHE'S A LADY WHO KILLED HERSELF IN ONE OF THE ROOMS AFTER HER FIANCÉ CALLED OFF THEIR WEDDING. SHE'S BEEN SEEN TRYING TO ENTER ROOMS WITH BAGS FULL OF STUFF, APPARENTLY BOUGHT WITH HIS MONEY AS REVENGE. THE ROOM SHE STAYED IN WAS NAILED SHUT FOR A WHILE, BUT SHE STILL SHOWS UP AND KNOCKS ON THE DOOR, TRYING TO GET IN. OR AT LEAST HER GHOST DOES.

NOTHING TOO SCARY — I MEAN, NOTHING THAT SOUNDS LIKE YOU'D END UP ZOMBIFIED FOR STAYING AT THE DRISKILL, BUT SOME PRETTY SPOOKY STUFF, NONETHELESS. SARAH NEEDS TO AVOID A VARIETY OF SPIRIT CREATURES AND THE HOTEL STAFF, FIND THE HALL OF MIRRORS, AND FIND THE FILM REEL. I HOPE SHE

DOESN'T KNOCK A MIRROR OFF THE WALL. THAT'D BE
BAD LUCK, AND WE SURE DON'T NEED IT.

THE REEL OF FILM WILL BE BEHIND THE TOP LEFT
CORNER, ACCORDING TO THE SKULL PUZZLE:

WOULD THE GHOST OF OLD JOE BUSH SHOW HIS
FACE AT THE DRISKILL? I DON'T THINK SO, NOT IN THE
LIGHT OF DAY, WHEN SARAH WOULD BE IN THERE. THAT
JUST SEEMS HIGHLY UNLIKELY.

FRIDAY, JUNE 24, 6:00 P.M.

WRONG! YOU HAVE GOT TO BE <u>KIDDING</u> ME. THE DRISKILL HOTEL HAS ANOTHER GHOST, AND IT'S <u>MY</u> GHOST, THE GHOST OF OLD JOE BUSH. SARAH GOT IN AND MADE IT TO THE HALL OF MIRRORS WITHOUT A PROBLEM. SHE FOUND THE MIRROR SHE WAS LOOKING FOR AND SHE GOT THE REEL OF FILM, WHICH WAS CAREFULLY HIDDEN BEHIND THE MIRROR. THEN SHE TURNED AROUND AND POINTED THE CAMERA AT THE MIRROR ON THE OTHER SIDE, AND THINGS WENT OFF THE RAILS.

YOU HAVE TO SEE THIS TO BELIEVE IT. PLEASE, JUST GO LOOK AT WHAT SARAH RECORDED.

THERE'S MORE ABOUT THE CROSSBONES — BUT MOST IMPORTANT, HE'S FOLLOWING HER.

THE GHOST OF OLD JOE BUSH WAS THERE.

SARAHFINCHER.COM
PASSWORD:
HALLOFMIRRORS

FRIDAY, JUNE 24, 11:00 P.M.

My day of work at the fly shop is over, I've put in some time with my mom on the porch, and Sarah is safely tucked away in San Antonio with her aunt. Tomorrow, Sarah will drive the entire day, fifteen hours to Phoenix, and I'll endure a Saturday at the shop, the only day when it's actually crawling with customers. The fish are biting, so we're going to sell a lot of flies and gear and give a lot of advice.

But none of that matters tonight, because tonight has nightmare written all over it. That video from Sarah was a bone chiller. Seeing the ghost of Old Joe Bush in that mirror, the way he moved, the way he whispered. It had to be real, right? I mean, there's no other answer. How else could it just show up like that? The only other answer besides TERRIFYING GHOST would be . . . I don't even know. Maybe there are secret rooms behind those mirrors where the Crossbones have their meetings and plan the demise of the human race. Who knows?!

A FEW THINGS I DO KNOW — SOME GOOD, SOME BAD:

— I DO NOT WANT TO STAY AT THIS HOTEL.
EVER.

— IT'S OFFICIAL: THE A-POSTLE WAS IN A
MAJOR FIGHT WITH THE OTHER LEADERS OF THE
CROSSBONES.

— THE SKULL PUZZLE THAT HENRY HAD IN
HIS POCKET WAS MADE BY THE A-POSTLE. HE
SHOWED IT IN THAT FOOTAGE. AND THE PUZZLE
LEADS TO SOMETHING BIG THE CROSSBONES
DON'T WANT FOUND.

— MY DAD IS NOT PART OF THIS ORGANIZATION,
WHICH IS A HUGE RELIEF. THE FACT THAT HIS
SECRET GROUP, USED TO PROTECT THE DREDGE,
WAS ALSO CALLED THE CROSSBONES WAS A
TACTIC USED BY THE A-POSTLE TO GAIN POWER.
IT WAS A WARNING TO CROSSBONES LEADERS —
EITHER GIVE HIM WHAT HE WANTED, OR HE'D
REVEAL EVERYTHING. LEAKING THE VERY
NAME OF THE CROSSBONES TO JOE BUSH WAS
THE BEGINNING OF A DANGEROUS GAME.

— And that dangerous game, I'm pretty sure, led to Henry taking him down to the river. They must have fought, because that event ended with the Apostle drowning. It also landed the Skull Puzzle in Henry's pocket. Only now the Apostle's puzzle has found its way to MY pocket, and I'm one step away from figuring out where it leads.

— And last, the word PORT, which I can now add to UNDER and GROUND. This confuses me a little bit. I still think wherever this thing is hidden is underground, but those three words together could be UNDER PORT GROUND or PORT UNDERGROUND or GROUND UNDER PORT. No matter how it slices and dices, these three words lead to a port of some kind, so we're talking near water.

I sure hope the Winchester House proves more helpful.

Sarah is convinced that all roads lead to Thomas Jefferson. The Crossbones hated him and wanted him destroyed. They tried to kill him and drove him into financial disaster. What else could they have done to ruin his life? That part remains a mystery, but I have a feeling we're going to find out more when Sarah arrives at the Winchester House.

The last stop on her whirlwind tour will be the strangest, and her timing couldn't be better. She'll sleep over in Phoenix at a hotel predetermined by her parents, and finish the drive on Sunday. She's expected in LA on Sunday night for check-in at the dorm on UCLA's campus, then the film camp starts Monday morning.

Our plan for getting Sarah into LA Sunday night is a little on the shaky side, and it involves cutting out of Phoenix very, very early. Here's how it's going to work:

— Sarah will go straight to sleep in Phoenix when she arrives there at around 9:00 p.m. tomorrow night (Saturday).

— She's going to get up at 4:00 a.m. and start driving. It's ten hours to San Jose, so she should be there by around 2:00 p.m.

— Back on the road by 4:00 p.m. for a slightly late but reasonable UCLA arrival at 9:00 p.m.

I'm tired, but I'm also afraid of whatever nightmare will be waiting for me once I close my eyes. I'd call Sarah, but she's asleep for sure. Fitz doesn't have a phone. My parents are out.

Another solitary late night in Skeleton Creek.

I really need to get a life.

SATURDAY, JUNE 25, 3:10 P.M.

Nothing much to note. Sarah is on the move, heading for Phoenix. We talked this morning and she sounded upbeat but just as confused as I am. She's excited about film camp, but she's even more excited about getting to the Winchester House and finding whatever's hidden at the top of a set of stairs that leads to nowhere.

I'm with her.

SUNDAY, JUNE 26, 9:11 A.M.

It's dreadfully quiet. Sunday mornings are like that in Skeleton Creek. At least I don't have to listen to Bon Jovi.

I'd write more, but there's nothing going on around here worth mentioning, and Sarah is doing pretty much nothing but driving and listening to music. She's bored, I'm bored. I bet even the ghost of Old Joe Bush is bored. Probably sitting in a tomb somewhere playing cards with some other dead people while we get our act together.

Sunday morning makes me think of the Apostle in a different way. The guy was nuts, for sure, or maybe just acting nuts, but either way, he went to church on Sundays. My parents aren't the churchgoing sort, but Sunday mornings are sacred in their own way for us. It's silent, for one, almost like everyone is tiptoeing around. And the porch is a favorite spot. While some people from town walk by with their Bibles in hand giving us sideways glances that say <u>you should be going to church, you heathens!</u> we just

SIT THERE DRINKING OUR COFFEE AND READING WHATEVER IT IS WE WANT TO READ.

It's spiritual in its own way. We do set the world aside for a few hours. We talk slower, quieter, nicer. And what is the church, anyway? My dad is fond of saying, "It sure ain't no building, I can promise you that," and this strikes me as a small but meaningful pearl of wisdom.

Me, I think heaven is on the river. It's where I feel my connection to whoever made all this stuff. It's where I find peace. Casting is my prayer, for what little it's worth. There's nothing more mysterious and beautiful than a wild fish in a mountain stream. It lives a secret life in a world I can never know, but if I can catch it, I can hold it in my hand for a moment. After that, I can bash its head in or let it go. As you might imagine, I let them all go. I don't want to upset the balance of nature.

This is what happens in Skeleton Creek when the world outside goes silent and my best friend is driving, driving, driving. I start talking about

THE MEANING OF LIFE, WHICH APPARENTLY HAS SOMETHING TO DO WITH FISH.

THE WINCHESTER HOUSE CAN'T SHOW UP FAST ENOUGH. A FEW MORE HOURS AND SHE'LL BE THERE. TOO BAD I'LL BE AT THE SHOP WITH FITZ WHILE MY DAD TAKES THE DAY OFF TO LOUNGE ON THE PORCH TAKING NAPS AND READING THE SUNDAY BOISE PAPER (IT'S A WHOPPER).

Fitz doesn't mind if I talk on the phone while I'm working, but I'm nervous about making calls to Sarah while he's standing there. He's a pretty aloof sort of guy, very focused when he's sitting in front of his fly-tying vise or reading up on some arcane casting technique, but still, I wouldn't want him knowing about what me and Sarah are up to. The fewer people who know, the better.

So it was kind of alarming when Fitz called me out.

"How's Sarah doing?" he asked me.

At first I thought he was just, you know, making small talk, so I brushed it off with a simple "Pretty good, as far as I know."

"Wish I had a cell phone. Dad won't get me one. Says it's too expensive."

"It is," I cautioned him. "Half the money I make in this place goes to covering my monthly bill."

"Must be nice to keep up with her on the road."

At first, this seemed like a normal-enough question. But then I wondered: How did Fitz know

ABOUT SARAH'S TRIP? I DIDN'T SAY ANYTHING, AND
FITZ LOOKED UP FROM HIS WORK ON A PERFECT
PARACHUTE ADAMS, A HARD FLY TO TIE JUST RIGHT.

"YOU KNOW YOUR DAD STILL WORRIES ABOUT YOU
GUYS," HE SAID. "HE TOLD ME HIMSELF."

SO THAT WAS IT. MY DAD WAS USING RIVER TIME
TO GET FITZ INTO THE LOOP, PROBABLY HOPING TO USE
THIS FLY-TYING FISH-FACE TO INFILTRATE MY WALL
OF SILENCE.

"LOOK, FITZ, MY DAD'S PARANOID AS ALL GET-
OUT. HE BLOWS EVERYTHING OUT OF PROPORTION.
SHE'S DRIVING TO FILM CAMP IN LA, NO BIG WHOOP."

"I'M THINKING MAYBE YOU'RE THE ONE WHO'S
PARANOID. YOUR DAD IS JUST WORRIED ABOUT YOU,
IS ALL."

OKAY, THIS WAS STARTING TO ANNOY ME. HE
COULDN'T OUTFISH ME, SO HE WAS TRYING TO BE MY
DAD'S BEST FRIEND?

BUT THEN HE WENT FOR THE JUGULAR, AND IT SORT
OF SHUT ME UP.

"YOU HAVE NO IDEA HOW GOOD YOU HAVE IT
AROUND HERE," HE SAID. "I BARELY SEE MY DAD, AND

WHEN I DO, HE DOESN'T HAVE MUCH TO SAY. HE COULDN'T CARE LESS ABOUT FOOTBALL _OR_ FISHING."

IT WAS THE FIRST TIME SINCE I'D MET HIM THAT I ACTUALLY FELT SORRY FOR FITZ. HIS DAD NEVER CAME AROUND. IN FACT, I'D NEVER EVEN MET HIS DAD. HE LOGGED UP IN THE FOREST FOR A LIVING, AND LET ME TELL YOU, CUTTING DOWN TREES PAYS EVEN WORSE THAN OWNING A FLY SHOP, AND IT TAKES EVEN MORE TIME.

ALL THE SAME, I STAYED QUIET ABOUT SARAH. TEXTING ONLY, WHICH WAS BIG-TIME INCONVENIENT ONCE SHE ARRIVED AT THE WINCHESTER HOUSE.

ME: CAN'T TALK, AT THE SHOP, FITZ IS HERE.

SARAH: YOU'RE SO MISSING OUT. THIS PLACE IS THE BEST. HUGE, WEIRD, AWESOME.

SARAH: AND THEY DON'T CARE IF I USE MY CAMERA!

ME: DID YOU FIND THE STAIRS TO NOWHERE?

SARAH: HOLD YOUR HORSES.

ME: I HATE THIS.

SARAH: PRICE YOU PAY FOR STAYING HOME.

ME: NOT FAIR.

SARAH: NEITHER IS DIGGING UP A GRAVE ALONE AT MIDNIGHT.

ME: OUCH.

SARAH: I'M PEELING OFF FROM THE GROUP. HANG TIGHT.

FOUR MINUTES WENT BY BEFORE SHE WAS BACK.

SARAH: THAT WAS CLOSE. ALMOST GOT CAUGHT.

ME: WHAT? DID YOU GET IT???

SARAH: I GOT IT.

AND THAT WAS IT. SHE HAD THE LAST CLUE THE APOSTLE HAD LEFT BEHIND IN HER HOT LITTLE HANDS, AND IT WAS ONLY 2:42.

AHEAD OF SCHEDULE.

LONGEST DAY OF MY LIFE. THERE IS NOTHING MORE FRUSTRATING THAN HAVING A REEL OF 8MM FILM SITTING IN THE BACKSEAT OF A CAR THAT YOU CAN'T WATCH UNTIL YOU GET TO AN OUTLET, PLUG IN THE DANG PROJECTOR, AND POINT IT TO A WALL. SO ANNOYING. SARAH HAD THE GALL TO DRIVE BACK TO LA FIRST AND CHECK INTO HER DORM ROOM. SHE WAS ARRIVING AT THE UCLA CAMPUS JUST AFTER 8:00 P.M. HER ROOMMATE WAS A LOCAL GIRL WHO WASN'T SCHEDULED IN UNTIL MONDAY MORNING, WHEN THE WEEKLONG CAMP WOULD BEGIN, SO THE ROOM WAS ALL HERS.

DURING THE NEXT HOUR SHE CALLED ME TWICE, ONCE TO LET ME KNOW SHE'D DONE ALL THE PLEASANTRIES AND LANDED IN HER ROOM SAFELY, THE SECOND TIME AFTER WATCHING THE LAST APOSTLE VIDEO. IN TYPICAL MADDENING SARAH FASHION, SHE WOULDN'T TELL ME WHAT IT REVEALED, ONLY THAT SHE'D FIGURED OUT WHERE THE LAST LOCATION WAS BY WATCHING THE APOSTLE. I BADGERED HER FOR INFORMATION, BUT SHE WASN'T HAVING ANY OF IT.

"Give me a few hours and you'll have your chance" was all she'd say.

I knew better than to push Sarah. If I texted her too many times for answers she'd make me wait until morning. She was a filmmaker and this was her big finale. For Sarah, spilling the beans on the phone would be like me reading the last page of a book while I was still in the middle of the story. I got that, but it didn't make me any less crazy.

I spent the next three hours staring at the Skull Puzzle and the map, wondering where this was all leading and how Sarah would get to the last location. One thing was for sure: It would have to wait a week, because there was no way we could spring her from camp now that she was in. We'd been incredibly lucky to get her there without finding our way into serious trouble.

At 11:30 p.m., a text message showed up on my phone.

Check your email. I'm a zombie — totally wiped out — me go sleep now.

I COULD HARDLY BLAME HER. SEVEN DAYS, FIVE THOUSAND MILES, AND FOUR HAUNTED LOCATIONS — SARAH HAD DONE TEN TIMES THE WORK I HAD, AND SHE DESERVED SOME REST BEFORE WHAT WAS SURE TO BE A GRUELING WEEK OF FILMMAKING.

I FIRED UP MY SARAH—ONLY GMAIL ACCOUNT AND FOUND HER MESSAGE.

Ryan,

I uploaded everything to my site in one chunky video as usual. The Winchester House had the best story of them all. I could have spent a week on that short documentary, but there just wasn't any time. You've also got the footage of me finding the reel, which was tucked into the edge of the stair. (I had to pry up a piece of molding, so hopefully I don't get busted somewhere down the road.) The Apostle is at the end.

I hate to be the one to tell you this, Ryan, but I think you're up to bat.

You'll see what I mean when you watch the video.

Zzzzzzz.

S.

What was THAT all about? I had a bad feeling the last location was going to be right here at home in Skeleton Creek, the one place I didn't want it to be. It would mean I'd be the one digging a grave at midnight or some other kind of unthinkable horror.

Unfortunately for me, the news was even worse.

Rainsford.

Nice password, Sarah. The main character from "The Most Dangerous Game," a short story we'd both read in the same junior high class a few years ago. We'd both loved the idea: Rainsford lands on an island and finds he's being hunted like a wild animal. Did Sarah think I was about to be Rainsford in our story? And if so, who was going to do the hunting? The Raven, Winchester's ghost, or some other creature of the night?

You'll have to watch the video to find out. That's what I had to do.

SARAHFINCHER.COM
PASSWORD:
RAINSFORD

MONDAY, JUNE 27, 12:14 A.M.

IT DOESN'T TAKE SHERLOCK HOLMES TO FIGURE OUT I'M IN BIG TROUBLE.

THE FINAL LOCATION IS CLOSER TO ME THAN IT IS TO SARAH. THOSE FOUR WORDS: UNDER, PORT, GROUND, LAND — COULD ONLY SPELL OUT ONE PLACE: PORTLAND UNDERGROUND. I WROTE THE WORDS ONTO THE SKULL PUZZLE AND STARED AT THEM:

EVEN IF WE COULD WAIT A WEEK, WHICH I DON'T THINK WE CAN, PORTLAND IS A SOLID FIFTEEN-HOUR

DRIVE IN THE WRONG DIRECTION FOR SARAH. THERE IS NO WAY TO GET HER THERE, EVEN AFTER CAMP ENDS.

So REALLY, IT WOULDN'T MATTER IF WE WAITED A WEEK OR A MONTH. SARAH WOULDN'T BE ABLE TO DO IT.

THIS TIME, THE TASK IS GOING TO FALL TO ME.

I'M GOING TO HAVE TO LEAVE SKELETON CREEK, MAKE THE SEVEN-HOUR DRIVE TO PORTLAND, AND FIND WHAT WE'VE BEEN LOOKING FOR.

I HAVE A BAD FEELING ABOUT THE GHOST OF OLD JOE BUSH ON THIS ONE. THE FIRST TIME I SAW HIM, I'D JUST GOTTEN DONE CLIMBING A LONG SET OF STAIRS UP INTO THE RAFTERS OF THE DREDGE. THIS TIME, IF HE SHOWS UP AGAIN, I'LL BE UNDER THE EARTH IN AN ANCIENT TUNNEL.

IT FEELS LIKE I'M ABOUT TO WALK INTO MY OWN GRAVE AND NEVER RETURN.

MONDAY, JUNE 27, 8:20 A.M.

I KNOW WHAT I NEED TO DO, BUT I SO DO NOT WANT TO
DO IT. I LEFT HOME EARLY THIS MORNING AND CAME
BACK DOWN TO THE CAFÉ TO THINK. TODAY IS GOING
TO BE BUSY AT THE SHOP, GETTING EVERYTHING READY
FOR THE TWO-DAY RIVER RUN. IT'S A TRIP I'VE
DECIDED I CAN'T MAKE, EVEN THOUGH THE THOUGHT OF
LETTING FITZ HAVE MY SLOT IS NEARLY KILLING ME.

WHAT CHOICE DO I HAVE? THE STARS HAVE
ALIGNED, AND EVEN THOUGH I'M BOUND TO GET INTO
SOME SERIOUS TROUBLE OVER THIS, I HAVE NO CHOICE.
MY DAD WILL BE GONE ALL DAY TUESDAY AND
WEDNESDAY. LATER TODAY HE'LL DRIVE MY MOM TO
THE BOISE AIRPORT SO SHE CAN FLY TO SEATTLE. SO
WHAT DOES THAT MEAN? IT MEANS I COULD BE ALL
ALONE TUESDAY AND MOST OF WEDNESDAY. NO ONE
WILL BE BACK AT THE HOUSE UNTIL EIGHT OR NINE
WEDNESDAY NIGHT. THIS IS PROBABLY MY ONLY
CHANCE.

I CAN'T BELIEVE I'M EVEN HAVING THIS
CONVERSATION WITH MYSELF. AM I HONESTLY WILLING
TO FAKE AN INJURY, GET IN MY MOM'S MINIVAN, AND
DRIVE TO PORTLAND? IF I DO THIS AND THEY CATCH

ME, I MIGHT NEVER DRIVE AGAIN. THEY'LL TAKE AWAY MY LAPTOP AND MY PHONE. MY RELATIONSHIP WITH SARAH WILL DRY UP IF WE CAN'T STAY CONNECTED, AND MY SUMMER WILL TURN ISOLATED AND LONELY. FITZ WILL OUTFISH AND OUT-FLY-TIE ME ALL SUMMER. IT WILL BE DEPRESSING.

AND ALL THIS SO I CAN COMPLETE AN INSANE JOURNEY.

IT'S AN AWFUL LOT TO RISK, BUT I'VE DECIDED IT'S WORTH IT.

NOW MORE THAN EVER IT'S PAINFULLY OBVIOUS THAT SARAH IS WORLDLIER THAN I AM. SHE'S IN LA AT FILM SCHOOL, FOR CRYING OUT LOUD. SHE JUST DROVE ACROSS THE ENTIRE COUNTRY! AND SHE'S RIGHT. THIS IS GOING TO BE GOOD FOR ME. SCARY, BUT GOOD FOR ME. I NEED TO GET OUT OF THIS PLACE, DO SOMETHING WILD. I NEED TO BE THE ONE WHO FACES HIS FEARS FOR ONCE.

I'VE PRINTED OUT A COPY OF THAT LAST SHEET OF PAPER THE APOSTLE HELD UP, AND I KNOW WHAT IT IS. IT'S HOW TO GET INTO THE PORTLAND UNDERGROUND AT NIGHT. IT'S HOW TO FIND WHAT I'M LOOKING FOR ONCE I'M DOWN THERE.

Here comes Fitz on his old motorcycle.

Time to put phase one of my plan into action.

It's good to make your friends happy once in a while, even if it means you'll be staring a ghost in the face for doing it. I limped out of the café and onto the sidewalk as Fitz pulled over. Blue smoke from the tailpipe drifted into my face and I about gagged. The combination of aromas from the café and his oil-spewing motorcycle was not the rosiest mix.

"Did you hook your toe or what?" Fitz asked me. I swear, Fitz CANNOT imagine anything in life not being somehow related to fishing.

"Fell down the stairs at home, reinjured it," I lied. I'd already tried this lie out on my mom and dad, and they'd both fell for it hook, line, and sinker. (Oh, no. I'm becoming Fitz. Note to self: No more fishing metaphors.)

"That's a bummer. Rowing for two days is gonna kill."

"Don't I know it — which is why I'm not going. Looks like you got the gig."

"No way! You serious?"

Fitz was beaming. There is nothing a trout bum loves more than leaving the world entirely behind and basically living on the river for days, not hours in a row. He was happier than I'd ever seen him before, which actually felt pretty good.

The good feeling went away pretty quick when I fake-hobbled back into the café and slumped down in my booth.

Was I really doing this?

How in the world did I even end up in this situation? Voluntarily giving up the best fishing trip of the year, lying to my parents, taking risks like I'd never taken before — it all added up to a serious case of the crazies.

Sarah and I were right back where we always ended up.

On the edge of disaster.

My mom is on a plane to Seattle. Her piece-of-junk minivan is parked in the gravel on the side of the house. The tires are pretty bald, which makes me nervous. Will that thing even make it to Portland and back?

Maybe I should take the bus.

MONDAY, JUNE 27, 3:00 P.M.

FITZ JUST TOOK OFF TO CLEAR THE TRIP WITH HIS DAD, WHICH MEANS HE'S GOING TO BE GONE FOR A WHILE. THEY CUT TREES UNTIL DARK JUST LIKE WE FISH UNTIL DARK, AND MY DAD'S LEAVING BRIGHT AND EARLY. FITZ KNOWS THE GENERAL AREA WHERE HIS DAD IS CUTTING, BUT NOT EXACTLY. HE COULD BE GONE FOR A FEW HOURS, DURING WHICH TIME I'LL HAVE TO GIMP AROUND THE SHOP AND WINCE IN PAIN AS MUCH AS POSSIBLE WHILE I HELP MY DAD PACK FOR THE FLOAT TRIP.

I HATE MAINTAINING A LIE ALMOST AS MUCH AS I HATE TELLING IT IN THE FIRST PLACE. EVERY STEP I TAKE IS A REMINDER OF HOW I'M FLAT—OUT DECEIVING MY PARENTS.

MY DAD IS GOING TO KILL ME IF I GET CAUGHT.

IT TOOK FITZ FOREVER TO GET BACK, BUT HE'S A GO.

EVERYTHING IS SET.

TOMORROW MORNING, MY DAD WILL DRIVE THE TRUCK TWO HOURS UP INTO A NO-CELL ZONE, ONE RAFT IN THE BED OF THE TRUCK AND THE OTHER PULLED BEHIND. HE'LL PICK UP FITZ ON THE WAY, SO THE OLD MOTORCYCLE DOESN'T GET LEFT IN FRONT OF THE SHOP HALF THE WEEK. THE TRUTH IS, I THINK MY DAD BELIEVES IF IT'S SITTING THERE WHILE HE AND FITZ ARE GONE, I'LL BE TEMPTED TO GO JOYRIDING ALL OVER TOWN. ACTUALLY, UNDER DIFFERENT CIRCUMSTANCES, THAT WOULD PROBABLY BE TRUE. I'D LOVE TO RIDE THAT THING, BUT FITZ IS VERY PROTECTIVE.

THE FOUR GUYS MY DAD IS GUIDING WILL FOLLOW IN THEIR OWN CAR, THEN THEY'LL SPEND AN HOUR DOING THE SONG AND DANCE TO MOVE A RIG TWENTY MILES DOWNSTREAM. UNLOAD THE BOATS, DRIVE BOTH RIGS DOWN, LEAVE THE TRUCK BEHIND. WHEN THE TRIP IS OVER, THEY'LL LOAD UP THE BOATS AND MY DAD WILL DRIVE UPRIVER WITH ONE OF THE CLIENTS TO GET THEIR CAR. I KNOW, COMPLICATED, BUT IT'S THE ONLY

WAY TO RUN TWENTY MILES OF RIVER WITHOUT A LONG WALK AT THE END.

THE LAST THING FITZ SAID TO ME BEFORE HE TOOK OFF FOR HOME WAS THANKS. HE REALLY DID APPRECIATE THAT I'D GOTTEN MY LEG ALL BENT OUT OF SHAPE JUST IN TIME FOR WHAT MIGHT BE THE ONLY OVERNIGHT FISHING TRIP OF THE ENTIRE SUMMER.

I COULDN'T BEGRUDGE THE GUY. I'D HAVE FELT THE SAME WAY, I SUPPOSE. BUT IT WAS A LITTLE LIKE WATCHING YOUR FRIEND GET INJURED IN THE BIGGEST FOOTBALL GAME OF THE YEAR SO YOU COULD TAKE HIS SPOT ON THE TEAM.

IT'S NOT THE KIND OF THING YOU SHOULD THANK SOMEONE FOR.

MY MOM CALLED TWICE TO CHECK ON ME, WHICH MADE ME FEEL LIKE A TEN-YEAR-OLD. SARAH'S RIGHT; I GOTTA GET OUT OF HERE. I'M SIXTEEN, NOT TEN, AND I'M SUFFOCATING IN SKELETON CREEK. SARAH WAS SMART TO GET OUT WHILE SHE STILL COULD. ME, I'LL PROBABLY BE RUNNING THE FLY SHOP AND SITTING ON THE FRONT PORCH FEEDING MY PARENTS SOUP THROUGH A STRAW WHEN I'M FIFTY.

THERE'S NO DENYING THE FACTS.

1) I AM LAME.

2) I'M TOO CHICKEN TO LEAVE TOWN AND I MIGHT NOT GO THROUGH WITH IT.

LUCKILY FOR ME, RIGHT WHEN I WAS FEELING MOST SORRY FOR MYSELF, SARAH SENT ME AN EMAIL. IT WAS MAYBE THE BEST EMAIL I'VE EVER GOTTEN IN MY LIFE.

Dear Ryan,

I was going to call you but I thought it would be better if you could have this in writing, even though writing really isn't my thing. First day of camp was fine.

Um, actually, I'm lying, and I can't lie to you.

The first day of film camp was awful. Everyone here is amazing, Ryan. What was I thinking, coming to this stupid thing? Did I actually think a small-town girl from nowhere could hold her own against people from LA, the film capital of the world? I kid you not, there's a thirteen-year-old kid here who understands filmmaking a billion times better than I do. His sample project was like *The Usual Suspects* meets *Paranormal Activity*, so you can imagine what the people in my own age group are bringing to the table.

Lighting, setting up, script writing, directing actors, angles, shot selection, tone — Ryan, I'm in big trouble here. I don't know anything about any of those things. I just point and shoot and cut and blend. Being here has made me realize something I never knew before.

I'm a hack.

Okay, end of pity party. Let's talk about you instead.

I know what you're thinking. You're not sure if you can go through with it. Well, you can. YOU, Ryan McCray — you can do this. Is there a chance you'll get in big trouble? Sure there is, but it's worth the risk. And you've earned the right to find whatever the Crossbones are hiding. Just think — if this leads to something connected to Thomas Jefferson, we could be returning something to the world that shouldn't be buried underground.

You could change the course of history. All it's going to take is a little courage and a minivan.

It's your time, Ryan. Don't let it pass you by.

Sarah

She's right; I can do this.

I WILL do this.

Tomorrow, life changes for me.

I'm leaving Skeleton Creek.

I wrote her back.

Thanks for inviting me to the first annual Sarah Fincher pity party.
I think about one of these a decade is enough, because Sarah,
you're going to blow everyone away. I'm sure of it. Give yourself
a day or two, be a sponge, take it all in. It's only going to make
you better. I predict you'll leave there at the top of the class,
because you have something a lot of people don't have: something
to say.

I'm getting in my mom's car in the morning and heading to
Portland.

Count on it.

R.

TUESDAY, JUNE 28, 10:00 A.M.

I KNOW, I KNOW, I KNOW! I SHOULD HAVE LEFT BY NOW.
IF I'M NOT CAREFUL IT'S GOING TO BE DARK BEFORE I
GET THERE AND THAT WILL BE A DISASTER. NO WAY
AM I GOING DOWN THERE ALONE AT NIGHT. I'M NOT
EVEN SURE I COULD GET IN THERE AT NIGHT. THE MAP
THE A-POSTLE SHOWED SEEMS TO INDICATE THAT I
COULD, BUT WAS DRAWN, WHAT, FIFTY YEARS AGO?
I DOUBT THAT ENTRANCE EVEN EXISTS ANYMORE.

LAST NIGHT I HAD A NIGHTMARE OF OLD JOE
BUSH FOLLOWING ME DOWN A CORRIDOR WITH AN AX. I
WAS STANDING IN BLACK TAR UP TO MY KNEES, TRYING
TO RUN AWAY, BUT HE JUST FLOATED CLOSER AND
CLOSER. WHEN I GOT DOWN ON MY KNEES AND FELT
THE TAR FILLING MY LUNGS, I WOKE UP COVERED IN
SWEAT. I WAS TOO AFRAID TO GET OUT OF BED, SO I
JUST LAY THERE SHIVERING IN THE DARK. A LIGHT
BREEZE BLEW MY CURTAIN AWAY FROM THE WINDOW,
AND I SAW HIM.

HE WAS THERE. IT WAS NO SHADOW OR TREE LIMB.

THE GHOST OF OLD JOE BUSH WAS WATCHING ME,
HIS HEAD BIGGER THAN EVER IN THE BLACK NIGHT. HE

WAS STARING AT ME WHILE I CLIMBED OUT OF A TAR-FILLED DREAM, WONDERING WHAT I WAS GOING TO DO WHEN MORNING CAME.

I TURNED AWAY AND COULDN'T BRING MYSELF TO LOOK BACK. I JUST LAY THERE, TEXTING SARAH OVER AND OVER: <u>HE'S HERE.</u> <u>HE'S HERE.</u> <u>HE'S HERE.</u>

BUT SHE NEVER ANSWERED.

SOMEHOW, AGAINST ALL MY EFFORTS TO STAY AWAKE, I FELL BACK ASLEEP IN THE EARLY MORNING BEFORE LIGHT AND DIDN'T WAKE BACK UP UNTIL MY DAD WAS POUNDING ON THE DOOR AT EIGHT, YELLING FOR ME TO GET UP. SKELETON CREEK WAS AN EARLY MORNING TOWN; IT WAS PART OF THE CULTURE. WAKING UP AT EIGHT WAS WHAT LAZY CITY FOLKS DID.

"I'M LEAVING IN FIFTEEN — LET'S GO OVER THE RULES ONCE MORE," HE SAID, OBVIOUSLY NOT PLEASED I'D SNOOZED SO LATE. HE DIDN'T TRUST ME WITH THE SHOP WHILE HE WAS GONE, BUT I WAS ALL HE HAD.

I WAS GOING TO LET HIM DOWN, THAT WAS A FACT, AND IT LEFT A HOLLOW FEELING IN MY GUT.

WHEN I SHOWED UP ON THE PORCH DOWNSTAIRS IN MY SHORTS AND A WRINKLED T-SHIRT, MY DAD GAVE me my marching orders for the millionth time. No driving, bring a lunch so the shop stays open, don't bug your mother.

"I don't think I'll have to worry about bugging Mom. I bet she'll call me ten times today."

It was true. She hardly ever left town, and I was going to be home alone. I made the mistake of following my dad as he walked down the steps of our porch to his pickup.

The limp was gone, forgotten in a sea of black tar the night before.

"Looks like your leg is feeling better," Dad said. Was he suspicious or just surprised? I couldn't tell.

"It still hurts, but yeah, it's starting to bounce back."

"Too late to change plans or I would, champ. Lay low, get better, we'll get you out there on the next one."

As my dad opened the squeaky door to his old truck, I felt a depth of guilt the size of the Hindenburg. He actually felt bad for me for missing out. He'd called me champ, a rare treat.

And I was about to deceive him big-time. Here he was leaving me in charge of the fly shop, and I wasn't even going to be here.

All I could think of at that moment was that it wouldn't be worth it. No matter what I found out there, I'd lose my dad's respect and trust in the process.

That's why it's taking me so long to pull out of the carport.

I'm sitting in the van, staring out the window. My hands are shaking.

I've been sitting here for almost an hour.

I'M LEAVING.

It's a seven-hour drive to Portland if I don't stop, and I just stopped. Sarah had her Steak 'n Shake, her Waffle House, her Cracker Barrel. Me, I'm at the Kmart loading up on everything I forgot. I packed food for the road, since the smell of fast food in a car makes me want to barf. I was so stressed this morning I forgot to bring a shovel. I loaded my backpack with every kind of tool I could think of: screwdrivers, files, a hammer, a hatchet (for protection against zombies and vampires), but I'd neglected to bring a shovel. I found a folding one for camping that fits in my backpack, grabbed one of the sandwiches I made and a Mountain Dew, and I'm heading back on the road. Should hit Portland by 8:00 p.m.

My mom is on schedule. She has called my cell phone five times.

I've lied each time. As far as she's concerned, I'm sitting in a fly shop in Skeleton Creek.

TUESDAY, JUNE 28, 7:00 P.M.

BAD, BAD, BAD, BAD NEWS! THIS VAN HASN'T BEEN MORE THAN AN HOUR OUT OF SKELETON CREEK IN FIVE YEARS, AND NOW I KNOW WHY. BECAUSE IT'S A PIECE OF JUNK! I'M STUCK AN HOUR OUTSIDE OF PORTLAND AT SOME GAS STATION ADDING OIL. THE ATTENDANT GAVE ME FOUR MORE CANS AND SAID, "SHE'S A LEAKER, BUT THERE'S NOT MUCH YOU CAN DO ABOUT IT UNLESS YOU WANT TO REPLACE THE TRANSMISSION, WHICH WOULD COST TWICE AS MUCH AS THIS THING IS WORTH."

HE TOLD ME TO STOP EVERY HUNDRED MILES AND POUR IN ANOTHER CAN, AND THAT I SHOULD BE PREPARED FOR THE WHOLE THING TO GO BELLY-UP AT ANY MOMENT.

NOT WHAT I NEEDED.

I CALLED AND TEXTED SARAH, BUT SHE'S LOCKED DOWN IN CLASS. ALL I GOT WAS THIS TEXT AT 4:00 P.M.:

PICK UP CELL = GET YELLED AT. STAY CALM! I'M OFF THE GRID UNTIL BREAK AT 8

PERFECT.

TUESDAY, JUNE 28, 8:30 P.M.

Just stopped to load a can of oil and use the bathroom. Last rest stop before Portland. The burning oil smell of the engine makes me sick. Either that or it's my nerves.

It's going to be dark in an hour.

At least my mom is at the Bon Jovi concert, where she'll stop calling me every hour.

It's the little things that keep a guy going.

TUESDAY, JUNE 28, 9:50 P.M.

Driving in traffic is — wow — harder than I thought it would be. I'm amazed I didn't plow right into the big river that cuts through downtown Portland. At least I got here in one piece and figured out how to parallel park. It helped that there were three spots in a row, but still. I have parked!

The trick now is getting out of the car, which I do not think I can do.

Oil is leaking onto the pavement. I can smell it. In my imagination, I can see it hissing as it hits the hot pavement.

I'll never forget that smell.

SARAH CALLED ME, OR I WOULD HAVE LEFT SOONER. NO, SERIOUSLY, I WOULD HAVE. REALLY, WHAT DOES IT MATTER? THE PORTLAND UNDERGROUND IS CLOSED, ANYWAY. IT'S DARK OUTSIDE. WHEN I GO IN JUST DOESN'T MATTER. MAYBE I'LL WAIT UNTIL MIDNIGHT, MAKE IT AS CREEPY AS I CAN. IF I'M GOING TO OVERCOME MY DEEPEST FEARS, I MIGHT AS WELL GO ALL THE WAY.

SHE ENCOURAGED ME IN THE BEST WAY SHE KNEW HOW: BY TELLING ME SHE WOULDN'T BE SURPRISED IF I TURNED FOR HOME WITHOUT EVER GOING UNDERGROUND.

I REMINDED HER THAT, TECHNICALLY, EVEN IF I COULD GET IN, IT WOULD BE BREAKING AND ENTERING. THE PORTLAND UNDERGROUND IS CITY PROPERTY. THEY GIVE TOURS DOWN THERE AND STUFF, SO IT'S NOT LIKE IT'S TOTALLY ABANDONED.

TUESDAY, JUNE 28, 11:53 P.M.

I couldn't do it. After staying in the car until almost 11:00 P.M., I walked the three blocks to Chinatown and realized, um, yeah, not a great place to hang around at night. Lots of shady-looking characters and all-night bars. And it gets worse. The place where the Apostle showed a secret entrance? There's a building sitting on top of it. It must not have been there fifty years ago, but this makes it official: I'm not getting in there unless I take one of the tours.

If something big is hidden underground, I won't be able to remove it without getting caught.

MORE BAD NEWS. IT'S PILING UP, WHICH MAKES ME FEEL MORE THAN EVER THAT I MADE A BIG MISTAKE COMING HERE. AFTER I MOVED THE CAR TO A TRUCK STOP ON I-5 AND ATE PANCAKES FOR DINNER AT THE ALL-NIGHT DINER, I DECIDED I BETTER ADD MORE OIL TO THE CLUNKER. MY HANDS GOT ALL GROSS AND I WENT FOR THE GLOVE BOX, HOPING TO FIND AN EXTRA RAG OR OLD NAPKINS IN THERE. WHAT I FOUND INSTEAD TOOK MY BREATH AWAY. I SAT IN THE DRIVER'S SEAT NUMB, UNABLE TO MOVE.

THERE WAS A CELL PHONE IN THERE AND IT WAS ON. I'D NEVER SEEN IT BEFORE, AND THERE WAS ONLY ONE REASON WHY IT WOULD BE IN MY MOM'S GLOVE BOX: GPS.

MY PARENTS HAD PUT IT THERE SO THEY'D KNOW IF I DROVE OUT OF TOWN. I KNEW HOW THESE THINGS WORKED. ALL A PERSON HAD TO DO WAS GO ONLINE AND PUT IN THE CELL PHONE NUMBER. IT WOULD SHOW WHERE I WAS WITHIN ABOUT TWENTY FEET.

WHAT A SINKING FEELING.

THEY KNEW WHAT I WAS DOING.

My mom, she knew where I was. She'd always known.

Maybe that's why she kept asking me: Where are you? What are your plans?

How many times had I lied to her while she sat staring at a hotel computer screen, knowing good and well I was not minding the fly shop in Skeleton Creek?

What a disaster.

On the off chance that she hadn't actually checked the thing yet, I turned it off. If it didn't work, they couldn't prove I'd gone anywhere.

Lies upon lies upon lies. It never stops with just one.

One is always just the beginning. Count on it.

WEDNESDAY, JUNE 29, 10:00 A.M.

The first Underground tour starts in an hour, and I'm parked a block away. At this point, if I'm extremely lucky, I'll get back to Skeleton Creek before dark. One flat tire and I'm hosed. My dad is picking my mom up at the airport at 8:00 p.m., then it's ninety minutes to the house.

9:30 p.m. is the latest I can go.

Wait until they find out I drove all the way to Portland and back. What a fun conversation that's going to be.

Signing off until I finish the task at hand.

Underground tunnels full of black tar, here I come.

WEDNESDAY, JUNE 29, 1:12 P.M.

HORRIBLE, HORRIBLE, HORRIBLE! IT WAS BAD DOWN THERE. HE WAS THERE.

I DON'T HAVE TIME TO WRITE, GOTTA DRIVE OR I'LL NEVER MAKE IT BACK IN TIME!!

I'M FREAKING OUT.

The unthinkable has happened, but at least I can take comfort in my journal, since I'm not driving.

Blow out. Fourteen hours on four bald tires — I should have known better.

This is going to set me back another hour while I'm stuck in Pendleton, Oregon. By some miracle I blew the front right tire next to an off-ramp and rolled right off the freeway into a gas station. The attendant told me I was a moron for driving a hundred yards on a flat. It's amazing what adults will say to a teenager. If it weren't for the fact that I was in such a rush and the tire had begun shredding off the rim, I'd have burned rubber right out of that place for the insult. Not that my mom's minivan can burn rubber, but I dreamt it could as I stared at this good-for-nothing mechanic. There were also six-foot flames shooting out of the tailpipe in my dream, which torched his stupid mustache off.

Ninety-two bucks and an hour — that's what it's going to take, which will leave me with barely enough gas money to get home.

Sarah knows everything. I told her already. She called in sick today and stayed in her room just so she could be there for me. What a friend — I mean, really. I hadn't done that for her even once on her long trek across the country. She said now she knows how I feel when she goes out and does crazy things. It's not as fun as she thought it would be. In fact, it was way worse than doing things herself — at least that's what she said. It was the first time we'd walked in each other's shoes, and I think we both had a lot more sympathy for the other from that point on.

I recorded bits and pieces of my harrowing trip underground on my phone. Each one was like thirty seconds or something, small enough to email. I sent them to Sarah while I was running to the car. It was the last thing I did before tearing out of Portland and hitting the highway for home. I didn't even know what was on those

SMALL FILES — IT COULD'VE BEEN NOTHING, BUT SHE POSTED THEM ALREADY. I THINK IT'S JUST IN HER NATURE TO CUT THINGS UP, MAKE THEM BETTER, AND PUT THEM ON HER SITE. SHE FELT BAD FOR ME, I COULD TELL. AND SHE WAS SCARED. I THINK DOING THE WORK MADE HER FEEL BETTER.

I WISH I HADN'T SAT ON THIS CURB AND WATCHED.

SARAHFINCHER.COM
Password:
MAGIC8BALL

When you're underground, it doesn't matter if it's day or night outside. It's cold down there, shadows bounce on thin light, and you can't stop thinking about how you're going to get out when the trouble starts.

I did a good job of losing the group when I realized where I was on the A-postle's map. No one seemed to care about the disheveled teenager who'd gone missing. The route the A-postle sent me on led quickly to a roped-off area screaming with no admittance signs. In that section the walls came in close and the light was almost nonexistent. I fished my flashlight out of my backpack and kept at it, twisting and turning as the ceiling got lower and lower. By the time I reached what appeared to be the last turn, I couldn't hear the tour guide's voice anymore and I was slouched over like an old man.

I was lost in a labyrinth of underground tunnels, alone in the dark.

Or so I thought.

Now that I'm sitting on the hot June pavement, staring at my phone and watching the video footage I captured, I realized something: I wasn't just having a mental breakdown.

The ghost of Old Joe Bush really was there. My paranoid brain didn't make that up.

He was sitting on a wooden crate, staring off to the side, moving in that otherworldly way he has — fast, then slow, then fast again. His voice was sand and dirt, as if it hadn't had a drop of water in a decade. And if I'm not mistaken, this thing had definitely turned benevolent. In other words, this ghost wanted to help me. It wanted to protect me. Who am I to care if it's Henry or some possessed version of Henry or not Henry at all? The point is, if I tell my dad or the cops or whoever, there's a chance me and Sarah might end up all alone out here.

And according to the ghost of Old Joe Bush, we're in real danger. Because this other guy, the Raven, doesn't mess around.

Apparently, we've upset him and he's out for blood. The fact that I found what I came for in the Portland Underground is a real problem.

I know this in part because of what I was told down there, but even more because of what I found down there, which I refuse to write in this journal until I get safely back to Skeleton. Creek.

I'm not even sure what it is.

All I know is I gotta get home and fast or I'll be grounded for the rest of my life.

Who am I kidding? When my dad finds out what I did, my life as I know it will be over.

WEDNESDAY, JUNE 29, 10:10 P.M.

One flat tire and a whole lot of oil later, I'm finally home. Unfortunately, I'm not the only person who's here. I've pulled off to the curb on Main Street and I can see my dad's pickup sitting in the driveway.

Is there a worse feeling than staring at your dad's truck, knowing he's inside, knowing you're in trouble? If there is, I haven't felt it.

It might be a while before I get back to my journal, and it's a fair bet they'll take my phone and my laptop the second I walk in the door. One last text to Sarah, then it's time to face the music.

I'm home safe. Hope to bust this thing wide open within the hour but I may not have a phone. Hold tight!

See you on the other side.

THURSDAY, JUNE 30, I DON'T KNOW WHAT TIME IT IS AND I DON'T CARE

I'M ALONE AGAIN, AND THIS TIME, IT'S A GOOD THING. A LOT HAS HAPPENED IN THE PAST TWENTY-FOUR HOURS, ALL OF WHICH I JUST GOT DONE TELLING TO SARAH. SO THAT'S THE FIRST THING — THEY GAVE ME MY PHONE BACK. IT'S FUNNY HOW FINDING SOMETHING INCREDIBLE — LIKE GOLD OR TREASURE — WILL COVER A MULTITUDE OF LIES AND DECEPTIONS.

WHEN I GOT HOME, MY PARENTS FREAKED OUT, BUT NOT IN THE WAY THAT I EXPECTED THEM TO. THEY DIDN'T YELL AT ME OR START TAKING MY THINGS — THEY DID THE OPPOSITE. MY MOM HUGGED ME, HARD, FOR A LONG TIME. SHE KEPT SAYING HOW SORRY SHE WAS THAT SHE'D LEFT ME HOME ALONE. MY DAD TOUCHED ME ON THE SHOULDER, AND WHEN I LOOKED AT HIM THERE WERE TEARS IN HIS EYES. I WOULDN'T HAVE IMAGINED THEY'D BE THAT WORRIED, BUT THE TRUTH WAS, THEY STILL HADN'T RECOVERED FROM ALMOST LOSING ME ON THE DREDGE. WHAT KIND OF CRAZY SON DID THEY HAVE? HOW MUCH LONGER WOULD I EVEN BE ALIVE? I'D MADE IT CLEAR I WAS A RECKLESS KID, UNTRUSTWORTHY, HEADING FOR THE ROCKS.

It was the first time in my life that I felt something deeper than guilt. I felt remorse. Remorse for making my parents feel as if they might lose me at any moment. They'd done a good job raising me, but I had to imagine that I was making them feel like they were the lamest parents on earth. What kind of parents raise a son who can't stop putting his life at risk?

The lovefest lasted about a minute, then the hammer came down and I was reminded that, yes, my parents did know how to discipline me. Not only was I going to have this new and crummy feeling of remorse for a while, I was also getting grounded and working at the fly shop with no pay until every hour I'd left the shop closed had been made up times ten (my dad's logic being that we'd lost a lot of sales while I was out joyriding). There were two places I could go: home and the fly shop. By some miracle of good luck, they let me keep my phone and my laptop, and for this I was incredibly thankful. Not being able to tell Sarah what was going on for days on end would have been impossibly hard.

After the hugs and the consequences, I came clean about Portland. I wouldn't call it squeaky clean, but I told them a lot. I did not, however, mention the road trip Sarah had been on and the many stops she'd made. I shortened my story by a long shot and stuck to only the facts I absolutely needed to share, which were these:

— I found an encoded message in the dredge, but I didn't tell anyone about it. (Technically, this is true.)

— The message has been lost, so I can't show it to anyone. Sorry about that. (This one is a stretch, unless you count "under my mattress" as lost. But I couldn't show the Skull Puzzle to just anyone. I had to keep it safe.)

— Part two of the message was hidden in Portland, which is why I had to go there. It felt important. (Again, technically true.)

— I found what I went looking for, and it led right back where I started: Skeleton Creek.

— The Crossbones is older and more mysterious than anyone imagined. They stole things and hid them. I think I may have found one of these things. (I did not go into any detail about the Crossbones. There was more to find, and I didn't want anyone trying to stop me.)

My dad was curious about a lot of what I'd said, but mostly, he was interested in one thing.

"What do you mean you <u>found</u> something?"

I could tell what he was thinking: <u>The last time my son discovered a hidden stash of whatever, it ended up being worth forty million dollars.</u> Maybe he was thinking about expanding the fly shop, I don't know, but his tone had changed. Ryan McCray, the guy who saved the town from ruin, had found something else. This could be good.

It was 10:40 at night, but I went ahead and set things in motion, anyway.

"We're going to need to talk with Gladys Morgan," I said.

"What in the world do you want with her?" my mom asked.

"She's got the keys to the library, and I need to get in there."

My dad was already pulling out his cell phone, looking at me like *What else do you need, son? Can I get you a Coke?* It was bizarre, but it gave me the freedom to really go for it.

"I'm going to need a crowbar and the biggest hammer you can find. An ax might be helpful."

"Honey, get the boy an ax," my dad said, and then he was at the tiny Skeleton Creek phone book (it was a pamphlet, really), dialing Gladys Morgan's home phone.

It was kind of hilarious when she answered. My dad had to pull the phone away from his ear, and even I could hear her yell, "Who in the blankety blank blank is calling me in the middle of the night?!"

There's something darn funny about an old librarian with a potty mouth. Even my dad was smiling.

We walked down Main Street carrying the tools we were going to need: I had the ax, my mom had the crowbar, and my dad had a sledgehammer. We must have looked like a gang in search of a midnight rumble. I imagined we were walking in slow motion, like in a movie trailer, which was just dumb enough to make me smile.

If Gladys Morgan was concerned when we'd called, she was downright out of her mind with worry when we showed up carrying tools of destruction.

"You're not coming in here with an ax and a giant hammer! Forget it!"

The time had come, there on the steps, to spill some of the beans.

"Gladys," I said, "your library has something very important in it. It's been there a long time, since before you showed up, and I think you'll be pleased if you let me rip the floor apart."

Gladys barred the door with her body and looked at my dad like his son had lost his marbles. We couldn't get her away from the

DOOR UNTIL MY DAD CALLED THE MAYOR, A KNOWN NIGHT OWL, AND TOLD HIM WHAT WAS GOING ON. MAYOR BLAKE IS MAYBE THE MOST OPPORTUNISTIC PERSON I'VE EVER MET, AND THE IDEA THAT SOMETHING ELSE OF SERIOUS VALUE MIGHT BE HIDDEN IN GLADYS'S LIBRARY WAS ALL HE NEEDED TO HEAR. THE BUILDING WAS OWNED BY THE CITY, HE HAD HIS OWN KEYS, AND HE WAS THERE IN UNDER FIVE MINUTES.

GLADYS WAITED ON THE FRONT STEPS, TOO DISTRAUGHT TO LOOK, WHILE MY MOM COMFORTED HER AS THE AX CAME DOWN. MY DAD IS ABOUT AS GOOD AS ANYONE I KNOW AT RIPPING THINGS APART, AND HE MADE QUICK WORK OF THE OLD FLOORBOARDS. ONCE WE HAD A HOLE IN THE MIDDLE OF THE SMALL ROOM, THE MAYOR WENT TO WORK WITH THE CROWBAR, PRYING UP BOARD AFTER BOARD. WHEN THE OPENING WAS FOUR FEET IN DIAMETER, WE WERE ALL DOWN ON OUR KNEES PEERING INSIDE.

THERE WAS A GIANT TRUNK DOWN THERE, TOO BIG FOR ONE GUY TO LIFT OUT, BUT THE ADRENALINE WAS PUMPING AND SO THE MAYOR AND THE FLY-SHOP PROPRIETOR OF SKELETON CREEK HEAVED IT UP INTO THE LIBRARY IN NO TIME.

When they opened it up, there was a severe case of disappointment written on both their faces. My dad looked at me as if I'd just bankrupted the family. The mayor was ashen. Not only had he destroyed a perfectly good floor, he'd almost certainly incurred the wrath of the cantankerous town librarian, a very bad move.

It was Gladys who saved me.

I pulled an envelope out of my pocket, the same size and shape and color as the one I'd found on the dredge. Only this one had been hidden in the Portland Underground for who knew how long. I took out the card inside and showed it to my librarian.

X marked the spot on the floor of the town library, with the words:

Jefferson Library, 287 volumes.

Gladys Morgan looked at the card, then the trunk of books, then the card.

If I didn't know better, I would have sworn she almost fainted and fell into the gaping hole we'd just created in her floor.

She pulled one of the books out — perfect condition — then another and another. She ran her weathered fingers over the spines.

The mayor, sensing all was not lost, ventured a question.

"Are you going to punch me, Gladys Morgan?"

She didn't answer. In fact, I don't recall how long she remained quiet, but eventually she broke her silence and smiled like I had never seen her smile before. It was the smile of a person who loved books and had found a rare and priceless treasure of words.

The Crossbones had tried to burn Jefferson's house to the ground. They'd tried to drive him into bankruptcy more than once. Those things didn't do him in, but there was one thing they knew he loved more than anything in the world: books. The Jefferson Library became the nation's library eventually, the very beginning of the Library of Congress. But to this day — almost two hundred years later — 287 books from that library had remained missing.

THE MOST PRECIOUS BOOKS OF THE 6,487-VOLUME COLLECTION HAD NEVER BEEN FOUND.

UNTIL NOW.

ME AND SARAH HAD FOUND THE RAREST COLLECTION OF BOOKS IN THE COUNTRY — THE MISSING BOOKS FROM THE THOMAS JEFFERSON LIBRARY — HIDDEN BENEATH OUR OWN CRUMMY LITTLE LIBRARY ALL THIS TIME.

YOU HAVE NEVER SEEN A PROUDER LIBRARIAN IN ALL YOUR LIFE.

COULD THERE BE A MORE PERFECT DAY TO REVEAL OUR DISCOVERY TO THE REST OF THE WORLD? I DON'T THINK SO. INDEPENDENCE DAY, OUR MAYOR CALLED A PRESS CONFERENCE ON THE STEPS OF OUR TOWN LIBRARY. GLADYS STOOD ON ONE SIDE, I STOOD ON THE OTHER, AND THE TV CAMERAS ROLLED. NOT ONLY WAS SKELETON CREEK HOME TO A HAUNTED DREDGE FILLED WITH GOLD, IT WAS ALSO THE RESTING PLACE OF THE NATION'S MOST-SOUGHT-AFTER COLLECTION OF MISSING BOOKS. WHAT WAS IT WORTH? PRICELESS, HE GUSHED.

THE BOOKS WOULD BE RETURNED TO THE LIBRARY OF CONGRESS AND THE HOLE IN THE FLOOR OF OUR QUAINT LITTLE ROOM OF BOOKS ON MAIN STREET WOULD NEVER BE FILLED. THE AX THAT FLEW AND CROWBAR THAT PRIED WOULD REMAIN RIGHT WHERE THEY'D BEEN USED. IT WOULD, IN TIME, BECOME A LOCATION AS IMPORTANT AS THE HOME OF THE LIBERTY BELL OR THE OREGON TRAIL. A TOURIST ATTRACTION EVERY FAMILY SHOULD SEE AT LEAST ONCE IN THEIR LIFETIME.

Mayor Blake really knew how to lay it on thick, which I suppose is a good thing to have in a mayor. I had a feeling he was going to sail through the next election without much trouble.

I felt bad about Gladys's floor, but she didn't seem to mind. Soon they'd move the library somewhere else and give her a real book budget. We might even get some books on tape and a computer in there, which, I had to admit, made me feel pretty good, too.

There was just one thing I didn't feel great about as people streamed up the steps to shake my hand. Sure, we'd solved a major mystery right under our parents' noses. And it was true we'd given something back to the world that had long been lost. But it didn't change the fact that Sarah was going to have to drive home in a few days. It didn't change the fact that the ghost of Old Joe Bush had given me one more envelope that night underground in Portland. It was a black envelope, old and marred at the edges.

Inside? Another puzzle.

Only this time, it was no Skull Puzzle.

In place of the skull was a black raven.

We'd made him angry, this Raven, whoever he or it was.

There were five more places to go, none of which I'd figured out yet, and Sarah was going to have to visit them on her return trip to Boston. It was the only way.

She'd find the ghost of Old Joe Bush out there.

She'd find the Raven out there.

And she'd uncover the last secret of the Crossbones.

My guess? Whatever it is sits right under our noses. All roads lead back to Skeleton Creek in the end, I'm sure of it.

But the most terrifying part of all? The part that will give me nightmares for weeks after?

I know who the Raven was, and I know what he carried around with him.

I figured it out that night, walking toward the library with my dad and my mom, carrying an ax that would rip open the past.

"Fitz never showed up for the fishing trip," my dad said as we walked. "He up and quit at the last second, left me high and dry. Longest two days of my life trying to guide four fishermen by myself."

Could it have been Fitz outside my window that last night before I left, watching me, wondering where I might go the next day? All I could think of the second Dad told me about Fitz was that smell. The smell of burning oil all the way to Portland. And then I knew: It was Fitz who had put the GPS phone in the glove box. (I'd asked my parents about it, and they had no idea what I was talking about.) He'd followed me all the way out of town on that crazy motorcycle of his. It was that bike of his I'd smelled, not my mom's junker. Thank God I'd lost him when I turned off that cell phone, because if I hadn't, who knows what might have happened in the Underground.

I might never have made it out of there alive.

MONDAY, JULY 4, 4:00 P.M.

I RODE MY BIKE OUT TO FITZ'S TRAILER, BUT I KNEW I WOULDN'T FIND ANYONE AT HOME. THE MOTORCYCLE WAS GONE AND SO WAS THE TRUCK FITZ'S DAD USED TO HAUL WOOD OUT OF THE FOREST. THE SORRY LITTLE MOBILE HOME WAS ABANDONED, BUT ON THE STEPS THERE WAS A FLY BOX, THE ONE FITZ ALWAYS CARRIED AROUND IN HIS FISHING VEST. I OPENED IT UP AND FOUND A NOTE INSIDE.

Ryan,

Maybe we'll see each other again sometime, but I doubt it. My dad, he asked me to keep an eye on you. He's not someone you say no to. I was supposed to figure out where you were going. I was supposed to take whatever you found and bring it to my dad. But I lost you out there. My motorbike isn't as fast as your mom's minivan. Not knowing where you were headed to might have been a good thing in the end.

But my dad was angry. <u>Really</u> angry.

He says we're leaving in the middle of the night and we're not coming back.

He says I failed to live up to the family name.

Look, Ryan, you don't know my dad. He's not a nice guy. I think you might have set him off.

Be careful. If I can swing a little help, I will. I'll find a way to get in touch.

Keep tying flies — you'll get better. It just takes practice.

Fitz

MY DAD WASN'T THE ONLY ONE CARRYING AN AX. THERE WAS A CERTAIN MAN OF THE WOODS, A LONER, A WOODCUTTER. THE DAD OF THE ONLY FRIEND I HAD IN TOWN.

A GUY WHO CALLED HIMSELF THE RAVEN.

THE LAST THREE CROSSBONES MEMBERS AT WAR: THE APOSTLE, HENRY, THE RAVEN.

ONE OF THEM DEAD, ONE OF THEM GONE OFF HIS ROCKER, ONE OF THEM AFTER ME.

THREE HIDDEN TREASURES: THE GOLD, THE JEFFERSON BOOKS, AND WHAT?

I wish I could say I know all the answers, but I don't.

I rode my bike back into Skeleton Creek, Fitz's old fly box in my shirt pocket, and thought about how far I was from safe.

My journey wasn't over yet.

SARAHFINCHER.COM
PASSWORD:
MISTERSMITHERS